A VAMPIRE'S HEART

AN ORDER OF THE BLACK OAK PREQUEL

MARIE-CLAUDE BOURQUE

SEA STORM PUBLISHING

A VAMPIRE'S HEART
An Order of the Black Oak Prequel
Copyright © 2022 by **Marie-Claude Bourque**
Sea Storm Publishing
P.O. Box 15531, Seattle WA 98115

Edited by Jennifer Bray Weber
Cover Design by Frauke Spanuth
Paperback ISBN: 978-1-956115-04-8

Vampires of the Black Oak
A VAMPIRE'S HEART - PREQUEL
A VAMPIRE'S SPELL
A VAMPIRE'S SIN
A VAMPIRE'S SOUL
A VAMPIRE'S FATE
A VAMPIRE'S STAR (2023)
A VAMPIRE'S BLOOD (2024)
A VAMPIRE'S CHRISTMAS - STORY (2023)
VAMPIRES OF THE BLACK OAK (1-3) (2024)

Warlocks of the Black Oak
A WARLOCK'S KISS
A SORCERER'S NIGHT
AN ALCHEMIST'S DESIRE
AN ARCHMAGE'S DESTINY
A SPELLBINDER'S DENIAL
A NECROMANCER'S LOVE
A WARLOCK'S STORM - STORY
WARLOCKS OF THE BLACK OAK (1-3)
WARLOCKS OF THE BLACK OAK (4-6)

"Bourque develops a world of mages and sorceresses unlike any other.
"

-- Night Owl Reviews
www.marieclaudebourque.com

To Logan and Finlay, for those Narragansett years

PROLOGUE

Ville-Marie, New France, 1751

"*V*alerian!" A muffled voice resonated outside his coffin—the unexpected sound jolting him straight out of the agony ushering every minute of what had felt like decades.

Darkness, it was all he could see. An all-consuming shadow so thick it weighted down upon his desiccated body. A constant companion to the bottomless solitude of his enduring penance.

"Valerian!" The call that had dragged him out of his persistent torment resounded again, clearer this time, bouncing off the stone walls of his hideout.

For *he* was Valerian Callan St-Amand, Mount-Royal Immortal and son of the infamous Ice Witch. He should have been living his unending years above ground with his five brothers, feeding yearly on human blood offered by his disciples at the *Rituel du Sang* ceremony. But he had chosen otherwise.

Beset with unfathomable shame, he had buried himself under the mountain at the age of eighteen, barely a man.

"Cahssare!" The incantation vibrated in the cavern, soon followed by a blast of crumbling rocks.

Seigneur. No. He clenched his weak jaw. Whoever this spellcaster was, he had managed to find Valerian's hiding place.

Entombed in a cave under Mount Royal, which shadowed the Ville-Marie settlement, he had been sealed within a thick wooden coffin of his own making. For how long, he didn't know, as he no longer detected time.

It had at least been long enough for his bones to throb with a relentless torture that had not left him since his blood had dried up. Every attempt to draw a breath had been met with a searing pain in his empty lungs, and a deepening of the torment that came with every movement, no matter how small.

This here was his penitence.

He had managed to convince Sasha Roussin, his best friend and brand-new assistant, to help him hide. The young Disciple of Nostredame had protested at first, using his weak magical knowledge in an attempt to fend off Valerian's compelling powers. But in the end, he'd had no choice.

With tears in his eyes, Sasha had sealed the lid of the coffin and blocked the entrance to the cave with boulders so that no one—not even Valerian's brothers or even Mother—could find him.

Valerian's parched throat closed in on his disgrace at the distant memory. It had pained him to the core to do this to his friend, but Sasha had been forced to take his secret to the grave.

The live burial was a fitting punishment for the horror of Valerian's crime. For the shame, the vileness of it.

With a simple ritual gone wrong, he had condemned a young woman to an existence as a monster, taking her natural life for something horrific none of them had ever encountered before—a vampire.

Pretty Emmeline, what did I do to you?

And the truth of his actions had come to him in a flash as he'd looked upon her hiding from the sun, snarling with blood lust over her first victim, her comely features smeared with the remains of her kill.

The fun-loving shopkeeper's daughter had been meant to be his wife. He had believed himself in love with her up until she'd turned into a hellish being. He had instigated the dangerous ceremony that should have made her immortal, wanting to be with her forever, but now, alone in his entombment with the timeless weight of his guilt pressing on him, he acknowledged that he'd been entranced by the pride of dating the loveliest girl in town.

They'd been both so young. And stupid.

"*Diable*, brother!"

Bleeding Hell. Valerian's feeble body lurched back at recognizing the holler striking his ears. Sasha must have revealed his secret to his family.

The lid of his coffin was suddenly yanked open, and he jerked weakly at the glow of an oil lamp burning his eyes.

His brother Justinien's familiar face hovered right above him.

"Valerian! What in the sacred heart have you done to yourself?" His kin considered him from behind a pair of iron-rim spectacles. Cool and self-possessed as he'd always been, the scholar was narrowing his eyes at Valerian with disbelief.

Filled with self-loathing, Valerian pulled his skeletal arm across his face to try to hide from his brother. "Let me be."

"Absolutely not, *mon frère*." Justinien pursed his lips with a curt nod. "It's time you return to the living."

"How long—" Averting his brother's disparaging gaze,

3

he wearily attempted to sit up and barely made it an inch before falling back against the coarse wood of his casket.

"It's 1751, brother. Long time."

"Sixty years?" Had he truly been interred that long? Each agonizing breath had taken forever. And yet he had spent over three generations hidden here as a living corpse. The memory of what he had done hit him full force. "Not long enough."

"Nonsense." Despite his stern tone, Justinien's features eased in the golden glow of the light dangling from his raised grip. "Much has changed since you locked yourself away. Including the death of Papa Antoine."

"Death?" A tide of grief clung to the back of his throat. "How on earth? Mother didn't make him immortal?"

"Papa's last breath was exactly one year to the day after you hid from us." The judgment returned to Justinien's voice. "It hit us all hard, devastated Magnovald the most. You should have been there for him. You two have always been close."

"But how could he die so young?" Valerian managed a trembling chin. The sorrow of hearing the news matched the pain in his wasted body. The weight of his guilt and self-loathing at not being present during this difficult time for his family suddenly became more profound.

Their father was a mortal man who had met their mother after her arrival from France as one of the so-called King's Daughters. Before she'd stepped foot on the ship, however, she'd been seduced and impregnated by a strange immortal being. But that hadn't mattered. Papa and Mother had fallen madly in love and together had raised the sextuplet boys.

"The disciples think it may have been rabies," Justinien explained. "Maybe the first case of this sort in *Nouvelle-France*. Papa was bit by a skunk during one of his hunting

4

trips. He was far gone when his companions brought him home and in one of his few lucid moments, he refused to let Mom interfere with her sorcery."

"He thought it would damn his soul to the devil," his brother added with a grim twist of his mouth.

"And our brothers?" With a dead ache in his soul from the tragic fate of his adopted father, he inquired further. "How are they all?"

"They're fine. Somehow withstood this immortality of ours." As he spoke, Valerian noticed that Justinien, despite being eighty-ish years old, looked like a man in his late twenties.

"Magnovald runs a public house," Justinien went on. "Cassiodore got into the fur trade but still likes to play the bard now and again. Renaud has taken over Papa Antoine's forge and Griffon decided he was more suited to uncover new territories. He's still away in the western lands he discovered in his last expedition with Monsieur Lavérendry."

Valerian took it all in. His brothers had moved on, old men now with different lives, while he had lingered in the past. He wondered if they all looked as young as Justinien.

"And you?" His jawbone creaked with pain at the effort of all this questioning.

"I run the seminary now. Recteur St-Amand, they call me." He chuckled a little with humility, reminding Valerian how his studious sibling had always brushed off his many academic awards when they were children.

Valerian nodded, still shocked to see his own brother standing there as if no time had passed between them. "How did you find me?"

"Took a while. Sasha had disappeared along with you and for a moment, once we found the note you had left for us on your bed, I thought you had buried him alongside you. But I know you are not that cruel." Justinien shook his head with compassion. "So I searched for him and I managed to track him down ten years later to a small village of the old country, but at the time he swore he knew nothing. He was an old man on his deathbed when he finally called for me this winter and told me where you were. Right next to us this whole time. I took the first sailing back to *Québec*. He must have departed this life mere days after I reached him."

"Poor Sasha. I was a rotten friend to him." Valerian's tired chest tightened with guilt. His best friend had been so proud to have been assigned as his assistant by the Guild of the Nostredame Disciples. And the faithful companion had been there until the very end.

It had been Sasha who had recited the mystical words that had condemned Emmeline, but it was Valerian who had instigated the ritual, forcing his companion to participate in her downfall.

A twinge of guilt hit him. He had not only doomed his fiancée to a terrible fate but his friend as well.

His remorse prompting him to act, he endeavored to push himself upward, a grimace of pain on his lips. Justinien set the lamp at his feet to assist him.

"You're a right mess, *mon frère*," he grumbled. "It'll take me a while to restore you."

"Restore?" He peered down at the emaciated limbs in his musty Sunday suit. His bony ankles rattled loose in the faded leather shoes. "Why? This is the state I deserve to remain in."

"*Diable*, brother!" Justinien fumed as he yanked on him. "I never took you for a coward."

"Coward?" He darted a glance at his sibling and frowned, deep in self-examination. "Maybe I *am* a coward."

He never did face Emmeline, never had the courage. He never went to his father who'd always been good counsel. And he'd been too ashamed to ask his mother to fix his mess.

"Oh no, Valerian. I won't let you wallow." Justinien tugged him upright and, with surprising force, lifted him out of the coffin and to his feet on the ground.

Valerian stumbled and held onto the damp stone wall of the cavern, breaking a thick spiderweb as he caught his footing. His brother's sudden outburst surprised him. Justinien had always been so composed.

"Do you know what's out there, *frère*?" Justinien intoned with frustration. "What you have unleashed by creating a *strigoi* creature?"

"Emmeline? She's not dead." How much more grief could he bear?

"Of course, she's not dead," Justin snarled. "Have you ever thought for one minute that what you have done to her went much beyond yourself?"

Valerian turned around to look at his kin and with a deep frown at his forehead, he leaned against his open casket on the stone bier. What was Justinien trying to tell him?

"Not only is she not dead, she looks the same as she did when you drained her."

"The same?" Valerian was still not following. How could she still be alive?

"Yes, the same. But a true monster underneath that beauty. She fed her way into sixty years of unending life and *created* more like her."

"More bloodsucking *strigoi*?"

"Yes. And as she does, they all feed, on *humans*."

"Like we do." He was still trying to understand, his brain not quite there yet.

"No, not like we do." Justinien smirked, showing the weariness of his burden. "Any bloody time they want. And sometimes, just for fun, they make *more*, exactly like them.

7

These predators are murdering innocents, even young children."

"So she didn't die," Valerian murmured to himself, filled with anguish at the revelation.

His guilt suddenly ran deeper. In running away and feeling sorry for himself, he'd given space for the problem to get so much worse.

"No. Maybe because you're immortal. I don't know." His sibling shrugged but his expression remained somber.

"And she still feeds on humans?" Valerian pursed his lips with sorrow.

"Not anymore. Not as often anyway," Justinien explained. "I managed to create some sort of imitation blood that pacifies her cravings."

Valerian's jaw set as the situation finally sunk into his skull. "You see her?"

"It's not like I have a choice," Justin countered with a wry face. "Papa Antoine told me to look after all of you. Why do you think I'm here?"

"Mother couldn't fix her?" In his long solitude, he had mused that she would eventually sort out this problem. She was the most powerful witch of the New World.

"Mother's gone," Justinien revealed. "We have not heard from her since Papa died."

"Gone?" Valerian shook his head in confusion. "Where?"

"First you left after turning Emmeline. Then Papa—" His brother stopped himself, his voice thick with sorrow. "And Mother took off the night of his passing. Our family was broken, and we could not find you."

Valerian attempted to straighten his spine despite the groans of his dry bones. These tragedies had happened while he hid away. His gut clutched at the heartache hitting him hard. His sorrow ran deeper than the physical pain of having wasted away.

Justinien must have noticed his wretched expression. His tone changed as he slid a supportive hand under his shoulder. "What were you thinking, brother?"

"I don't know." He winced. He'd been so craven, it was shameful.

"That maybe if you ran away from our lives, all would be better?"

"Maybe."

"You were young." Justinien lifted him upright to assist his steps. "You didn't know."

"You were the same age, and you knew. You told us not to do the turning ceremony." The memory of Justinien shouting and pleading with them to stop was still branded in his mind.

"Yes, well, I *did* take the time to read a few grimoires back then." His sibling tried to lighten the mood with a half-smile. "Seemed important to know these things."

Valerian gently pushed away from Justinien to stand on his own. His weak muscles hardened with the firm intention to right his wrongs. "I *have* to go back and face them all."

"There's no one to face, Valerian. Everyone you knew is gone. It's just you and our brothers."

"Emmeline?" What had become of her? Had he condemned her to a horrific end?

"And Emmeline." Justin's gaze turned inward as his expression became wistful. "Love… The things people do for love. You two had it hard for each other."

"Love? I don't know." Valerian searched his heart. It was only now that he realized that his love for her hadn't run that deep. If he had truly loved her, he would have done what he could to help her. Not run and hide. "I suppose we were playing at love."

"Some game," Justinien scoffed.

"Yeah." Valerian stumbled again under his feeble legs,

dislodging small crumbling rocks on the cavern's treacherous ground.

"Oh, by god, brother." Justinien swooped in to catch
him with a solid arm around his back. "I better fix
you up."

"I truly don't deserve your help." Valerian was
adamant.

His brother snorted. "I'm not having you return in this
state."

"Why did you even come look for me?" Valerian
protested.

"You're my brother, Valerian," Justinien stated. "It's my
duty to look after you."

He huffed. "Duty."

"Well, if you had done yours, we wouldn't have the
town run by vampires," Justinien pointed out with obvious
insight. "But here we are. We need to fix this. Together."

Valerian attempted to straighten his spine, collapsing
against his brother's sturdy grip, and was again overrun by
remorse. "I'm sorry, brother."

Justinien didn't answer. Instead, he steadied him
against the coffin and took a step back.

"Lisaquiren kolipas feòal a." He intoned the incantation
with a flourish of his hand. *"Lisaquiren kolipas oash."*

Warmth surged through Valerian's body and his breath
suddenly became less strained. His brother was healing
him, causing a curious sensation that he had never experienced before.

"Lisaquiren kolipas," Justinien repeated, using the
magical words learned from their mother as children.

Valerian felt his strength return to his limbs and he
stood upright with relief, no longer exhausted at each
exertion.

"You'll need human blood." Justinien slid his haversack
off his back and searched through the contents.

"How close to December are we?" The immortal brothers were fed a cup of their disciples' blood each year on the twelfth of December, a date that their ancient protector, astrologist Michel de Nostredame, had declared a crucial cosmic time for the holy blessing that kept them sane in their eternal life.

"It's spring, *mon frère*. The ice cover has melted on most of the mountain. Otherwise, I would have had trouble digging down here to reach you." He passed Valerian a flat glass saddle flask filled with a thick dark liquid. "Here, drink."

"What is this?"

"Imitation blood," Justinien explained. "It will have to do until we find you a new disciple."

"This is fake blood?" Valerian swirled the strange substance with a frown.

"I made it for Emmeline."

Valerian took a hearty swing, relieved by the familiar metal taste coating his tongue. "So, you do see her."

"She's around town," Justinien's tone stayed casual.

"And the beasts she created?"

"Crawling underground during the day," he cringed, "preying on people at night. The citizens know not to leave their dwelling when the sun goes down."

He drank more artificial blood and remained quiet for a moment, pondering Justin's words while listening to the sound of dripping water at the back of the cave. It was indeed spring, he realized. Snow was melting.

Now filled with sustenance, the bottle empty in his hand, his bearings and the path ahead for him turned crystal clear.

"I have to repair all of this." He returned the flask to his brother with a renewed sense of honor. How could he have stayed hidden here for so long when he was needed above? "Not sure how yet, but I will."

"I know, brother." Justinien's gaze connected with his, their familial bond still strong. "Come."

Valerian nodded solemnly as he straightened himself to his full height. Justinien tried to support him, but he stopped his sibling's attempt with a gentle palm. He could do this. He could walk into the sunlight after sixty years of cowardice and face his shame.

Together, they walked out of the cave under the mountains, disturbing ancient spiderwebs and small earthworms churning in the soil, each step bringing Valerian closer to his renewed life.

As they emerged into the Mount Royal's forest, Valerian was greeted with bright sunlight, fresh buds on the trees, and green shoots poking through the last patches of thawing snow. He stopped to survey the newly bustling town below—a mere fortified settlement when he had left it decades ago. He turned to the brother who had cared enough to come fetch him.

"I swear to you, *frère*, I *will* fix this." He held his head high as he stared at the vibrant woodlands surrounding him. He had made a huge mistake once, but never again. "I will corral every one of those beasts and right my wrongs."

"You have a long journey ahead, Valerian," Justinien commented as they followed a deer path along the mountainside.

"I know." He nodded, understanding fully the challenge now facing him. But nothing would dissuade him from his mission.

"You may want to see a certain Marguerite d'Youville and her Grey Nuns."

"A nun?"

"She's in the business of looking out for lost souls," Justinien continued. "She will know where to start. And our family house is still there for you. I'm at the seminary and Magnovald has a place above his inn. But Cassiodore and Renaud are still there. They'll be glad to see you."

"Thank you." Valerian impressed a grateful look on his brother, excitement emerging inside him at the thought of seeing them all again.

"It's what I do," Justinien told him with a heartfelt smile.

A tide of warmth radiated in his chest for the first time since the lid of his casket had closed in on him. Yes, he vowed, he would make it up to all those he hurt.

Especially to his ex-fiancée. The love may have been gone, but he owed it to her to give her the peace she needed.

Wondering where exactly she was, he paused at the mountain's flank to let his gaze trail down along the walls of the city, the wooden construction now entirely replaced by sturdy stones.

"Ville-Marie has changed so much," he mused out loud. "It's big."

"We call it Montreal now," Justinien said with pride. "A real city, with over four thousand souls. Twenty thousand if you count the small villages on the outskirt."

As Valerian scanned the rooftops, he could see a healthy number of new church steeples rising above thousands of chimneys joyfully smoking straight up in the frisky springtime sky. Birds darted above him at the edge of the forest, the tiny creatures chirping happily in search of a mate, while squirrels scampered along on the fresh meadow at his feet. Spring had burst onto Mount Royal in full force and love was in the air.

With a stab of regret, he acknowledged that love was what had created the trauma he had put everyone in. And so, it would no longer be for him, no. What he wanted was a lifetime of penance. Away from the treacherous desires of the heart.

As they approached the city's wall, a mongrel dog who had been napping by the entrance jumped up and down with delight, barking at them in greetings. He scooted toward Valerian, his tail flipping with eagerness at the newcomers.

"Hey, *copain*." Justinien absentmindedly patted his head as he passed by the animal.

Valerian crouched down to the dog's level. As he scratched him behind the ear, he felt an instant sensation of calm. "Where's his owner?"

"Oh, I don't think he has one." Justinien shrugged. "I've seen him wandering around town and begging for food scraps all winter."

Valerian dug his hand into the matted fur and the dog proceeded to lap his parched face with happiness.

"Are you all alone, boy?" Valerian beamed with warmth at the joy running inside the animal. The poor mutt would make a fine companion in his journey of atonement. His arm around the neck of the animal, he looked up at his brother as a feeling of peace washed over him. "I'm going to keep him."

"Why not." Justin smiled benevolently. "He seems taken with you."

"Sasha," Valerian said, filled with a transformative sense of purpose. "I'll call him Sasha."

CHAPTER 1

Berwick Hollow, New England
Late June, Present Time

Maisie Thibodeau sat in the dark, hunched over her tablet at the counter of her family's craft shop. The store had already closed but she hadn't moved, relentlessly going over Cousin Jo's spells.

"Honey, still studying?" Her mother walked in and turned on the light. She picked up Maisie's empty teacup and disappeared back behind the beaded curtains of the store's backroom.

Willow bark and black salt... Maisie was hard in concentration trying to remember the components of a potion to ward off evil.

"It's Friday night, sweetie." Mom returned and leaned her hip against the pine countertop right in front of her daughter. She fiddled with the plain gold chain at her neck. "You should be out enjoying yourself. The White Reaper has a band playing tonight. Your cousins will all be there."

Acacia root bark, crushed calendula flowers... Maisie's mind was still on the magical brew. Her grip tightened on her electronic device as she endeavored to brand into her subconscious the sequence needed for the concoction.

"Maisie!" Mom called more forcefully. "You'll wreck your eyesight looking at that screen day and night. This modern version of the White Holly's Book of Shadow is not natural."

Maisie smiled at the familiar critique and turned away from the spell for a moment. "It'd be the same if I used your old grimoire, Mom. You know I wouldn't stop studying."

"Uhm." Her mother's brows drew together but her features softened. She stepped in closer to gently stroke Maisie's back. "You're still nervous about the high priestess thing."

"Yep." Her stomach churned at the task laid out for her and she unconsciously gripped the pentacle at her neck. Mom's instincts were never wrong. The idea of taking over from her grandmother still didn't settle well with Maisie.

"Your mind is spinning again." Her mother's tone remained kind as she picked some invisible lint off Maisie's T-shirt. "Much too focused on your worries and ignoring your physical needs. We talked about this."

"I can't help it, Mom." Maisie drew a breath before letting it out with frustration. "That's how I am. Once I lock in on a subject, I forget everything else."

"And what did we teach you?" Mom asked patiently, rubbing her palm on her plain jeans.

Maisie didn't have time for this conversation. She was dying to look at the spell again. She kept forgetting one ingredient.

But Mom was right. She'd been so engrossed in her studies today, that she was neglecting her basic needs. She hadn't had anything to eat since breakfast.

She rubbed her eyes and suddenly noticed the tension

at the front of her skull. She never understood why, but as soon as she focused on something, she wouldn't let it go until she knew everything perfectly.

She reluctantly pushed the tablet away and looked at her mother.

"Turn it off." Mom grabbed one of the health bars they sold in the shop next to the old cash register. She placed the small shiny packaging in front of Maisie. "And eat something."

"But there is so much to learn," Maisie protested as she peeled off the wrapping from the snack.

"You still have a few months until Samhain."

"I'll never be ready." Her confidence faltered and she put the bar down without eating it. She was meant to take over as high priestess from Nana Thibodeau, her grandmother, who would present her as her successor to the ancestors at Samhain when the veil between the worlds was the thinnest. Such an honor, but also such a crippling responsibility.

"You will be ready, baby." Her mother offered her a genuine smile, filled with compassion. "It's all in your blood."

But Maisie couldn't shake off her anxiety. "Why isn't Nana passing the leadership of the coven on to you first?"

"I'm not the witch you are, honey. I never was." Her mom shook her head with conviction. "Remember those wraiths you took down last year with your cousin Ava? I can't do that. My ascent would not keep Aunty Beaudry satisfied. Or those annoying Cajun witches down south. Esmeralda has wanted to join our covens together for years. Having me at the head would give her an excuse to do it, claiming we're not strong enough by ourselves."

"Maybe it should go to one of the Beaudrys," Maisie countered. "Ava is one powerful spellcaster."

Her cousin was not only one of the most talented witches in their group, but also Maisie's closest friend.

"She can't. The high priestess of the White Holy coven has always been a Thibodeau. The Beaudrys, with this immortality they seek, makes them too unstable. No, they choose to risk their sanity to the immortal path, and we lead. It's been such since our days on the shores of Acadia."

Everyone in town tiptoed around the few immortal witches still lingering among them. There was cankerous Agnès Landry who lived in the woods at the edge of Berwick Hollow with her enchanted remedies that could cure most ailments. And the ethereally beautiful Daisy Arsenault who ran the dance studio on the main street. And of course, no one could forget The Elder, Aunty Beaudry.

Nana's great-aunt was a short and stooped crone straight out of a children's book with her long flowy black skirts and fringed shawl from the Old World. Rarely seen in town, she nonetheless had advised every high priestess since the late nineteen century.

There were more, naturally, but most disappeared somewhere in the forest behind a mystical barrier after a generational lifetime. Perhaps to remind the coven that the immortal path ended in some sort of coveted blissful existence, no matter how risky the ceremony was.

"Nana is pushing me into this too fast, Mom." Filled with conflicted thoughts, Maisie rearranged the assortment of paint brushes in the clay pot in front of her. "You know it, too."

"It's this parley." Mom shook her head. "Your grandmother and Aunty Beaudry need a show of strength in front of Esmeralda and those warlocks. They want to be able to present you as her next in line."

"I heard there will be banshees there tomorrow." Her

mind racing with the responsibility of her destiny, she tried to anticipate the summit.

"Apparently, yes, one or two of the old Davenport sisters will be there."

"I've never seen banshees." She went over the list of supernaturals she'd heard were coming. Druids, selkies, and even a panther-shifter.

"Walking alongside Death like this, they're a cranky bunch. But I'm actually more concerned about that darned Devereaux woman. Esmeralda will be here with some of her cronies from their Waxing Crescent coven."

"You expect problems from the Louisiana witches?"

"Maybe, and those vampires make me anxious." Mom leaned back on the counter with her arms crossed at her chest. "It's one thing to ally ourselves with the warlocks from Seaport and the Greystone druids, but vampires, I'm not sure."

"You mean the St-Amands. Aren't they more like immortal beings?"

"Has my mother told you about them?"

"Yes, luv. I told her." Nana Thibodeau suddenly walked in on them from the back room, regal as ever in her signature silk suit and pearls. "Maisie has to know all the details of who will be there. She'll soon run things in my place."

"I still think she's too young." Mom pursed her lips with worry.

"Nonsense, Clara." Nana ambled over to Maisie and placed a proprietary hand over her shoulder. "Maisie is twenty-five years old. I was younger when I took over from my own mother."

"Panthers, druids, the Waxing Crescent coven, vampires, those huntsmen from Seattle, who else will be there," Mom asked. "I sense trouble."

"You do?" Nana's tone softened as she slowly nodded

with genuine concern. "You were never a powerful witch, lovey, but you *are* a great empath. What exactly are you sensing now?"

Maisie frowned at her mother. "You never said anything about actual trouble."

"I didn't want you to worry. And for all I know, during this parley, you just need to stand quietly behind us with your cousins in that new summer dress I bought you, while the twelve leaders confer. It should be over quick."

"I *do* want to officially present her as my successor." Nana lifted her chin with purpose, her fancy updo still firmly in place.

"Have you told Aunty Beaudry of your plan?" Mom asked. "Does she agree that Maisie will be ready in four months?"

"Agatha still has doubts." Nana seemed to mull over the complications. "But if Maisie is to be presented in front of the whole council tomorrow, she will be accepted by default. How's your studying going, Maisie?"

"It's going." She turned the screen of her tablet back to life.

"Mother, you're pushing too hard." Mom's brows drew together, and she went back to fussing with her gold chain.

"The girl is a natural," Nana countered. "You're much too protective, Clara."

"She's strong at magic but a sensitive soul under all that academic bent."

"Mom, I'm right here!" Maisie faced her mother with sincere warmth despite her protest. She loved the women in her family, but they tended to take over her life. No wonder her dad often took off to study magic from other cultures around the world.

"If they don't accept you, you'll be crushed for days." Maisie's mom idly rearranged the sachets of beads in the cheery display by her side. She narrowed her gaze at her daughter. "Remember that jerk who took you out and never called back?"

"That delivery boy?" Nana eyed her daughter. "The one you put a spell on?"

"Well, he hurt my baby girl." Mom let out a forceful breath.

"We're not supposed to use magic to injure people," Maisie said. "Harm ye none, and all that"

"Lucky you're the high priestess's daughter," Nana told Mom with a twinkle at the corner of her eye. "You did break our coven's laws with that hex."

"It was self-defense," Mom explained to Maisie. "You were devastated, and in no position to retaliate. And the boy is fine now."

"He had just stopped calling me, Mom."

"After he took advantage of you, honey," her mother countered.

The truth was that he had indeed been devious. Taking her virginity in the back seat of his car, professing a love he did not feel. She'd been distraught for months after he'd brushed her off when she called him after their night together. Having Mom turning him impotent for a year had actually made her feel a little better. But she could not condone this kind of action against mortals, no matter how slimy.

"This is not the eighteenth century," she protested. "I was willing."

"Willing? You're too naïve, my child," her mother added. "He took advantage of the fact that you have never been out of Berwick Hollow."

"I went to college," Maisie rectified as she slid herself down from the cashing counter stool to plant her sneakers steadily on the floor.

"You went to class," Mom corrected. "You never experienced college life. You came back here every night."

"Too many strangers on campus." With a grimace, she turned back toward her tablet, avoiding her mom's worried gaze. She did in fact truly hate leaving her small town. "I don't do well with crowds when I don't know the people there."

"My point exactly." Her mom tugged at her plain white T-shirt with agitation before letting the matter drop. She turned to Nana. "Our town is overflowing with outsiders right now. We should never have accepted to have this parley here."

"Diesel Stanford insisted." Nana's confidence was reflected in her calm tone as she mentioned the leader of the Order of the Black Oak who had requested this summit between supernaturals.

"That young warlock means well, but I do actually sense trouble." Mom let go of her shirt to rearrange the yarn collection on the back wall with restlessness.

"It'll be fine, Clara. Thank goodness Maisie didn't inherit this nervousness from you."

"She's just like her father, all in the mind." She stopped fretting with the display and cast Maisie a fond smile.

As was common in witches' matriarchal families, Maisie was given her mother's surname—especially as the Thibodeau was a bloodline of high priestesses and she was destined to follow in her ancestors' footsteps—but she had indeed inherited her studious streak from her father.

"Where is Edwin, anyway?" Nana inquired.

"Still out in Argentina," Mom said. "Studying."

"Uhm," Nana griped. She did like Maisie's father—a descendant from a warlock family but possessing little magic himself—but she tended to bicker with him constantly just out of habit.

"What is that look, Mother?"

"He should be here with all that's going on," Nana huffed.

"Nonsense. You know he likes to escape this closed-in little town once in a while." Mom turned to face Nana and planted her hands on her hips. "We should have joined him, shut down the shop for a few weeks, get away from this whole parley thing."

"Maisie has to be here with me," Nana insisted.

Mom cocked her head to the side as she peered into Maisie's eyes with wariness. "That *is* what you truly want, honey, is it? Become our high priestess and run this place?"

"There isn't anyone else." Maisie leaned back on her heels with resignation. "Cousin Davina is much too young. And the Beaudrys, well..."

"Ava will soon be going through the immortality ritual." Nana glowered, showing her objection to the undying path. "Aside from the fact that it would be unheard of for a Beaudry to take over, an immortal witch would not be a sound and stable choice for a high priestess."

"She doesn't want the immortality," Maisie said. "We talked about this. She wants to leave Berwick Hollow."

"Really?" Nana brought a hand to her pearls in surprise.

"Yes," Maisie nodded. "She's under way too much pressure from Aunty Beaudry."

"That poor child," Mom said.

"It's why you girls will never do this wicked ceremony," Nana said with force. "It's not healthy to live so long. And there's too much risk, that poor little Sara Landry, she's still catatonic after a decade. She never recovered."

"So much power, though," Maisie said. There was no doubt that despite the risk, the ritual bonded them with a very primal source of magic, something so old, they had forgotten the very name of its power. Maisie couldn't help but be curious about how it would feel to have those kinds of abilities.

"Don't even think about it," Mom warned, catching

her dreamy look. "Nothing is worth the risk of losing your mind if the ritual fails. It has happened too many times in the past. Your aunt—"

"You're powerful enough, child." With a shake of her gold charm bracelet, Nana waved her hand to stop the reference to her departed older sister who had turned so mad from the immortality ritual that she'd eventually taken her own life. The brief painful shadow that crossed her eyes was swiftly repressed. "At least strong enough to counter whatever Agatha has in store for you this weekend."

Maisie flinched back. "What do you mean in store for me?"

"That's why I came to the shop. To warn you," Nana said. "Agatha wants to test you."

"What on earth?" her mom exclaimed.

"Test me?" Baffled, Maisie's throat tightened. That didn't sound good at all.

"To show if you are worthy of taking over," Nana continued. "Not sure when and why, but she'll put a situation in front of you and see how you do."

"Situation? How?" Maisie asked.

"Oh, I don't know." Nana shrugged. "She'll conjure up a few things. You'll just have to dispatch them. Some wraiths maybe, or another kind of monster."

"And you're telling her now?" Mom didn't like this any more than Maisie did.

"I just found out." Nana shot her a pinched expression. She, too, was annoyed.

"Cripes." Maisie was not prepared for this.

"Just be ready, that's all." Nana shook her head, a smirk twisting her classic features. "She'll probably want to do this when there are people around."

"I should just hunker down here, then. Continue to

study for the Samhain ritual until this so-call test comes to me."

"No, luv. You must go to the White Reaper tonight. Be seen." Her grandmother sharply rearranged the elegant scarf draped over her navy summer suit. "This test has to happen in front of everyone. They'll see you succeed, and no one will question your leadership."

"What happens if I fail?"

"Nonsense, you won't fail. You're as powerful as I am," Nana said. "You did get rid of those nasty wraiths trying to take over your high school during your senior year, didn't you?"

She shuddered remembering the fight. Two of those wretched beings had erupted in the gym during an evening basketball game and she had managed to help destroy them with a few well-placed incantations, her instinct taking over. There had been recordings. Everyone in town had seen them and had since acknowledged her skills as a crafty magic-user."

"So why do I still need a test?"

"Well, it's not just the town, it's the whole supernatural world. The warlocks included."

"Oh, by the triple Matronae," she groaned. She hated being at the center of attention. If she could run away to live her life as a hedge witch, she would. But she *was* a Thibodeau. Her duty was to the White Holly coven.

"What happens if I do fail?" she asked again.

"Well, Esmeralda would surely bring back the idea of merging our covens, which absolutely will not happen on my watch." Nana's brows were tight with righteousness. "And there are the Seaport warlocks. The Stanford matriarch is a witch, and so is that sister of Diesel, Celeste. That girl is assembling her own little coven. We can't have the warlocks hold dominion over us if they think we are weak."

"And Ava—"

"Out of the question." She pursed her lips and lifted her chin, stiff with determination. "She can advise you, but I will not have a weak-minded immortal witch lead my coven."

Mom sighed. "That's a whole lot resting upon her shoulders."

"Look Maisie, I know you don't do well in crowds and that you don't feel comfortable being in charge." Nana was now facing her, and she rested both palms on her shoulders as she dropped a steady gaze on her. "But there is one thing you are the best at, and that's being a witch. *You* are one of the most talented spellcasters I have ever seen."

Maisie gulped at the compliment. She was gifted, but was she that skilled under pressure?

"Agatha has been around for nearly a hundred and fifty years," Nana continued, gripping her shoulders with conviction, "and she does agree with me. But she would not be doing our coven justice if she didn't test you first. It's been a while since you took down those wraiths, and you did have Ava's help. People need to see you in action alone now. She'll expect you to shine so we can get all these outsiders off our backs."

Maisie inhaled deeply, filled with a sense of legitimacy at the task laid before her by her two elders. They counted on her. She could not let them down.

"Imagine what it'd be like to be a witch at the beck and call of others," Nana pressed on. "When those conquerors took over our Acadian lands and set us adrift on the ocean, some of our witch ancestors were kept back like pets to predict the outcome of battles. This shall never happen again. Our powers belong to us and us alone."

"I see, Nana." Maisie nodded, despite her rising apprehension.

"I have all my trust in you." Nana's lips curled into a

fond smile, and she let her go with a kind pat on her arm. "I know you will be superb. Just do what you were born to do. You will stay here in Berwick Hollow, lead the witches as you were meant to do. You will never need to leave this town, just as you always wished."

Maisie breathed and looked at her tablet for a moment, her heart racing at the upcoming challenge Aunty Beaudry had in store for her. She forced herself to stay calm, reviewing the next few hours to gather her wits and courage. She would go to the White Reaper bar, see her cousins, and battle whatever she had to fight with all she had.

"I won't let you down, Nana," she finally said. "I promise."

"I still think it's a lot on her young shoulders," Maisie's mom chimed in.

"Then you watch out for her. You, too, have power, Clara," Nana replied. "You've been too busy living your mortal life to use them to the fullest."

"Empathy is a burden, Mother." Mom narrowed her eyes. "Not a gift."

"It's okay, Mom. I got this." Maisie reached out for her mother's arm to comfort her.

She knew that Mom relied on Dad to stabilize her ramping emotions. Emotions that she had a hard time regulating being overwhelmed with feelings from others. Maisie was her total opposite, often having difficulty reading what people needed from her.

But here they were, three generations of mystical women holding on to each other. And this time, their survival and the safety of their whole coven depended on her, Maisie.

She was thinking of all the possible monsters Aunty Beaudry could conjure when the shop's bell jingled as the door opened to the outside air.

Cripes! Was this it already?

She swallowed with dread and—palms behind her with a defensive spell at the ready—she turned to the newcomers.

Her heart froze. She'd been totally unprepared for what she saw.

Flutters tumbled at the bottom of her belly as she stared at the two tall men blocking the entrance, a stout chocolate Labrador standing between them.

Both outsiders were darkly handsome with a family resemblance in the strong jaw and walnut-brown curls. Her eyes locked onto the one clad in a long dark trench coat over classic black pants and a knit shirt. Heat flushed up her chest as an inexplicable attraction took hold of her.

She eyed them with caution. Were they part of those huntsmen from Seattle? Definitely not Greystone druids. They looked much too young.

The one wearing a leather jacket over jeans shot her a fast smile and advanced to the counter. The other, still sending her heart racing, stayed by the door. His palm rested upon the dog's head as his brooding stare took in the store's displays.

"Sorry if you're not open but we saw the light." The friendlier man was right across her counter. A twinkle lit his eyes as he took her in and trailed his gaze over her small, fitted T-shirt.

"Can we help you?" Her mother had moved right in front of Maisie by pure instinct. She was reading their energy.

"Passing through town?" Nana smiled with a hand on Mom's shoulder as if to tell her to let Maisie handle this. If this was a test, so be it.

"We're looking for Diesel Stanford." The charming man turned to Nana. "We were told he'd be at the White Reaper bar, but we can't seem to find the place.

Maisie swallowed as she kept her scrutiny on the silent man at the door, wondering what it was about him that made her so uneasy. Fae? Daemon? Or just a plain rogue warlock from out of town? If an attack came, surely it would be from him.

"Bar?" she answered absentmindedly, still ready to defend herself if needed.

"Sorry but the place is not getting picked up by our GPS," the stranger at the counter continued.

"Oh, yes," she said, finally turning to him. She knew very well that a magical barrier made it difficult for outsiders to find their way by common modern means. No one ever came to Berwick Hollow unless they knew exactly where they were heading. "It's just a quarter of a mile down this road, a little to the left."

"Thank you, *fille*." He shot her a flirting glance. "And why aren't you there yourself? I was told the place is hopping on a Friday night."

"She'll be there shortly," Nana answered in her place while Mom remained quiet with an attentive look on her face. "Aren't you, Maisie?"

"Maisie, you say." The corner of the stranger's eye crinkled in appreciation. "Pretty name."

The mysterious man poised at the entrance still hadn't said anything. And yet, she couldn't help but be drawn to his heavy energy.

"Maisie Thibodeau," she answered with her head held high while her gaze still lingered on the handsome outsider who continued to stand aloof next to his dog.

"Ah." The charmer in front of her shrugged in his leather coat. "Thibodeau, you're one of those witches, aren't you?"

She was taken aback. "You know about us?"

"Of course." He extended a hand to her with a broad,

agreeable smile. "St-Amand is the name. You can call me Mag."

Oh, cripes. This was one of those immortals from up north. She shook the offered hand and found it cool but not cold. A pleasant shiver ran through her at the sturdiness of his grip.

"This over there is my brother Valerian. And his dog Sasha."

The mysterious St-Amand gave her a curt nod, not meeting her eyes.

"*Allez*, brother," Valerian St-Amand ordered, a slight accent coloring his speech. "Let's get on with it."

The rich tone of his voice warmed her down to her very core, making her even more flustered by his presence in her shop.

"My apologies for his rudeness, ladies." Mag nodded at her. "My brother just hates being out of Montreal."

She heard a snort from the door and caught the dark look Valerian cast his sibling. Yet he remained still, his palm calm and still gentle at the top of the dog's head.

"You're from Montreal?" she asked, not wanting to send them both on their way quite yet.

"Born and bred," Mag assured.

Born. How long ago must that have been. Centuries, if what she'd heard was true. And witch-born, too.

"I met your mother once," Nana told him. "Powerful woman."

"When she shows up." A dusky shadow crossed Mag's features, quickly repressed as his laid-back expression returned. He eyed Maisie again. "You should come to the tavern. It'd be nice to see a friendly face."

"She will," Nana said. "Aren't you, luv?"

"I guess." She pressed her lips together. She wouldn't escape this public test of hers. And a part of her deeply wanted to further observe those two immortal brothers.

"So down the street and to the left, you said?"

"Yes."

"Let's go then, Val." He turned away from the counter to join his sibling and patted the dog on his way to the exit. "Come on, Sasha Boy."

Valerian still hadn't said a word to her or caught her gaze as he turned his strapping shoulders to the glass door.

"See you there, then, *poupée*," Mag drawled over his shoulder.

But she had eyes only for his silent brother. Something in him called to her. The man was hurting. She could feel it in her bones. Her heart hummed with a strange frequency at thinking about the secrets hiding under that composed appearance. Maybe she did have some of her mom's talent after all.

She bit her lip as she watched them jump into a state-of-the-art jeep on the other side of the storefront window under the store's cheery fairy lights.

"So, you're going to the White Reaper after all?" Mom let out a slow exhale as if she'd been holding her breath the whole time.

Maisie tightened her fists, her emotions tumbling inside her from the unexpected encounter. She was dying to know more about these St-Amand immortals from Montreal. Desperate to hear his lush voice again.

She tried a casual shrug as she turned to her mother, attempting to hide her raging turmoil from Mom's keen perceptions.

"I am," she replied, her upper lip stiff with resolve. "I have no choice now."

CHAPTER 2

"*W*ell, here we are." Val turned off the ignition and stared at the bright neon sign hanging above the wooden porch of the local bar. The name of the establishment flashed orange and blue under the coarse glowing replica of a grinning reaper holding a giant scythe. He turned in his seat to the back of the Jeep where Sasha had dropped his chew toy as soon as he'd detected the motor dying off. "What do you think, boy?"

Ready to jump out, Sasha bolted to all four on the car blanket, his tail flapping with excitement.

"A bit of a dump if you ask me." Mag smirked as he peered at the place through the windshield.

"Mag…" Val smiled genially as he took in the rows of motorcycles and parked cars lined in front of the place. Nothing fancy, but not grungy either. His brother was so proud of his own club, a Montreal nightlife landmark, that he measured every other against his own.

"Look at that, the edge of the porch is peeling off. And these band posters are so ancient." Mag was pointing at the bar with animation as he leaned forward in the passenger seat.

"Well, the *Serpent* is not up to code, either," Val countered. Mag's place was still built on the foundations laid out centuries ago.

With mild curiosity, Val watched the glazed front door adorned with beer ads open to a middle-aged man stumbling on the steps. The customer stopped to pull his pants over his round belly before ambling over to a green Ford Fiesta that had seen better days.

"At least my clientele is classy." Mag raised a brow at Val as if the patron leaving the bar proved his point.

"Classy?" Val grinned at his brother's outfit of a plain black tee under his well-worn leather jacket. "I didn't know you went for classy."

"The women, man." Mag's gaze lit with lust. "The women."

"Yeah, I guess," Val agreed as he thought of the *Serpent Maudit's* head waitress Sandrine Dion running the show in her alluring outfits, and of the striking dancers permanently on display at the back podiums next to the fully-stocked bar. Clients were attractive and dressed in the latest fashion of the year, the bouncers making sure to only accept those who fit in with Mag's idea of luxurious desires.

But Val wasn't interested in women at the moment. He had his hand full with keeping Emme in check. It was enough to remind him that relationships weren't for him. He'd tried mirroring Mag's lead in pursuing casual encounters, but their emptiness had left him with a bad taste in his mouth.

These few affairs had only fulfilled a physical need that didn't satiate the hollowness within him. He had given no part of his heart to his willing partners. He was unworthy of a more meaningful relationship and besides, there was always the risk that he could be making another colossal mistake.

So he endeavored to be more like his brother Justin who had been celibate for as long as he recalled, after the natural passing of his mortal wife in the eighteenth century.

"Speaking of women," Mag grumbled, "why were you so rude back there?"

"Where?" Val wondered.

"At that Crafty Sprite shop. With those three women."

"Was I rude?" He was not quite following. His mind mulled over what was waiting for them in the bar. Would they finally meet Diesel Stanford? Val hoped his ally Mal Dunsmuir would already be there. He'd befriended the necromancer just a few months ago when Emme had stepped out of bounds and caused big trouble in Seattle.

"You barely said hello to them," Mag insisted.

"Was I supposed to chit-chat?" Val shrugged. He hadn't paid attention as Mag had turned on the charm as he always did with strangers, especially those of the opposite sex.

"They are *witches*," Mag said. "Isn't it what we're supposed to do here? Make friends with the enemy."

"They barely count as enemies," Val chortled.

"I wouldn't underestimate those three," Mag countered. "I could feel their power humming. Especially the little one."

"Which little one?" He remembered that one of them did seem younger, with a pleasant voice filled with hesitation.

"Behind the counter," Mag said. "Don't tell me you didn't notice her. Under those jeans and geeky T-shirt, she's all woman. Those green eyes, all that jet-black hair."

"The kid?" Val dismissed the attractiveness of the young woman swiftly, not willing to entertain it.

"She's a whole lot more than a kid, Val. She's a grown-ass witch, and a powerful one at that."

"I didn't feel anything." Val shot Mag a quick side look, repressing the hint of curiosity he had felt at hearing her state her name. *Maisie Thibodeau*, he recalled. A pretty name that was also weighted with ancestry. Wasn't the high priestess of the coven in this town a Thibodeau? They had to be related.

"You were standing back too far," Mag huffed. "Plus, I do notice these things."

"You're obsessed with everything magical, brother. All those artifacts you collect. It's what got us in this mess in the first place."

"You *were* rude, Val. Admit it. You're annoyed."

"Of course, I'm annoyed," he groused, pinching his expression. "It's all your fault we're here."

"My fault? "

"If you didn't have the Impervious Medallion in your safe, Emme wouldn't have been able to steal it and give it to some random cursed vamp. That banshee baby would never have been attacked in Seattle." The little girl was fine now, thank the heavens. But that mistake had revealed the Mount-Royal Immortals to the whole Order of the Black Oak.

They'd done a damn fine job keeping hidden from most supernaturals. But being powerful immortals invited unwanted trouble and unwarranted adversaries just by existing.

"Emme gave it to Evan, Val. She's *your* responsibility."

Sure, Val was guilty to some degree, but he would not let Mag off the hook, either. The medallion was incredibly powerful and gave the one who yielded it the ability to cross any warded threshold. Which was how Emme's protégé Evan had been able to enter the baby's nursery despite the seal of protection erected by three crafty old banshees.

"You could have guarded your trinkets a little better,"

Val admonished. "You don't need all those artifacts, brother. You have magic in you. Our mother's magic."

"She's no longer my mother," he spit the words out.

"Oh, come on."

"She left us in the middle of our grief, thinking only of herself." The deep disapproving grooves upon Mag's forehead were unmistakable.

"She was hurting—" Val was about to say more but stopped himself. He'd had contact with their mother since he'd returned to the living, but he didn't want to tell Mag, who refused to see her side. This was something they'd have to sort between the two of them.

"So were we," Mag ground out. "We needed her."

"We have each other." Val tried to appease his brother's obvious angst.

"Except you weren't there, Val." Mag winced, the circumstances of their father's death obviously still inhabiting a huge part of his soul.

Remorse flooded Val at remembering their losses.

And Mag was right. Emmeline was his responsibility. She had turned Evan Grant, a poor drug-addled street kid, and had taken him on a joy ride to Seattle where he had attacked that banshee baby. Val had managed to retrieve her and Evan to bring them back to Montreal and in the process had met Dunsmuir, the Necromancer and King of the Daemon World. The dark warlock had no issues with the existence of the St-Amand brothers as they both shared a mutual respect. But he'd told Diesel Stanford about them, and the leader of the Order of the Black Oak wasn't as unbothered. The fact that Mag stockpiled magical artifacts did not sit well with him at all. Hence, this parley.

Val understood his need for all of them to get along. Malcolm had told him it had taken months to get the White Holly witches on board. The coven liked to remain under the radar and had basically retreated from the world and only reluctantly accepted an alliance with the Seaport warlocks. The witches had finally caved as the world became more connected, seeing that banding together may ensure their survival.

But Val didn't have to enjoy being forced to make the trip down to New England for some council meeting.

"You're right, Mag," he confessed, staring again at the bar likely filled with their future allies. "I *am* annoyed. I don't want to be here."

"Another of Emme's messes to fix." Mag sympathized with a slow shake of his head. "Justin did a fine job at that centuries ago when you were away."

"Right. Good on Justin," Val said partly grateful, and slightly frustrated that their studious brother always seemed to be right. "I still think he should be here instead of us."

"Oh, I don't mind." Mag shrugged with his hand on the Jeep's door, ready to step outside. "I think it's fun. Ren said the warlocks even called on the wolves. He might be here to represent the Domaine-Lassalle wolf pack."

So even their brother Renaud was getting roped into this. Val rose a tired brow at Mag's enthusiasm. "You find this thrilling?"

"Meeting new people, like that cute witch at the shop? Yeah, sure." Mag opened the door an inch which caused Sasha to push his nose with eagerness between the two front seats. "And I was told the Davenport banshees will be there. I've never met a banshee. I heard they're all gorgeous, some with a telltale streak of white in their hair. They walk with Death itself."

"Do you ever think of anything besides seducing women?" Val's mood lifted at witnessing his brother's taste for life.

"Do you think I can compel a banshee?" he eagerly asked.

"I don't think you can compel anyone here, bro, sorry."
Val snorted with amusement as he patted Sasha's neck. His
brother would never change.

"*Sacrament.*"

"You have to do it the old-fashioned way."

"I can be charming."

"Oh, I know you can." Val was feeling more upbeat
now. Mag always brought out the best in him. Probably
why they got along so well. "Might want to avoid any trouble, though. Meet this Stanford warlock, then find a place
to stay. We should see if there is space at that B&B Father
Grégoire found for us."

"A B&B, how quaint. If all goes well, I'll find my own
place to sleep tonight, if you know what I mean."

"Mag…"

"Look man, I know you're desperate to run back to
Sanctuaire to fix that new batch of young vamps, but I have
not had a break from the club in years. This is fun. Maybe
that little witch will be there."

"And fall for your charm?" An odd sensation rose in
him at the thought of Mag seducing that young
Thibodeau witch further. He wished his brother would
leave her alone. She was truly not his type.

"Exactly."

Val forced himself to focus on what waited for him in
Montreal. Mag was right, Val wanted to be back at the
Sanctuaire des Truants with his elder disciple, Father
Grégoire, to continue his work with Evan's rehabilitation
and help reform the crew of new vampires that Evan had
created before heading to Seattle with Emme.

She hadn't touched a single soul since Malcom had
come all the way down to his city to emphasize she'd have
the Daemon World after her if she created more vampires.
But she had turned many in her centuries of existence and
no matter how many of her offspring Val hunted and

reformed, more could always be found. This new set had been nesting all the way over in Quebec City, hiding under the stone walls of the old town.

"We better go in." Mag fully opened the vehicle door to the warm night before jumping down to the gravel of the parking lot.

"Right." Val followed as he called on his dog. "Come on, Sash. Let's see if you can make new friends."

Sasha easily hopped to the front of the Jeep before following his owner outside. He lifted his nose up in the air with curiosity, smelling the unfamiliar scents of the town.

They crossed the distance to the establishment. As soon as he pushed the door open, Val was hit with a whiff of yeasty beer and the stale smell of too many people packed into a small space.

While Mag's club was indeed polished with an upscale urban clientele, this was a small-town joint. Not sleazy but a friendly local pub with its two waitresses in practical shorts and T-shirts, busily darting between small groups of people gathered at heavy rounded tables.

He noticed the band was taking a break by the bar, the stage empty aside from the equipment left behind for the next set. Piped-in classic rock played in the background.

"Hey bud," someone by the entrance said. "We don't allow dogs in here."

Val turned to the guy, a young doorman in a leather vest and white T-shirt and shot him a look so dark he flinched back.

"Sorry, sir."

"Where's Stanford?" Val went straight to the point. He wanted to meet the warlock who had summoned them and be out quick.

"Diesel Stanford," he added at the bouncer's puzzled look. "I was told he'd be here."

"I don't know anyone by that name, sir." The man cast

an eye at the patrons. "But this weekend is full of strangers, with that parley and all."

"Maybe the bar," Mag suggested, taking his eyes off the table by the door hosting a small party of attractive young women, their copper-hued hair glistening with an unnatural shine. Selkies, maybe? This place had to be crawling with supernaturals.

"Right." As they made their way through the busy establishment with Sasha at their heels, Val took in a gathering of bearded middle-aged men at a table. Three fierce males in fatigues sat at a nearby spot with a redhead clad in somber business attire. Chelsea Jones, their human leader, he recalled from his time in Seattle. And her huntsmen.

He leaned into the counter signaling to a young man serving drinks. The barman approached them as soon as he saw Val try to catch his attention.

"What is it gonna be?" he asked with an easy-going smile, placing a cork coaster in front of Val.

"Diesel Stanford," Val asked again. "Is he here?"

"Stanford, huh?" He nodded before shaking his head. "Not yet. I was told he'll be here tomorrow."

"Tomorrow?" Val gritted his teeth with frustration. "I was hoping for tonight."

"Must have been held back."

"Could be that hot wife of his." An older man sitting on the barstool beside him chuckled. "Couldn't stay away."

"Wife?" Mag stopped ogling the waitresses to turn to the customer.

"She's one of them, a panther." The stranger nodded at a table further back where a handsome couple chatted ignoring the crowd. Their heads were close together, the blonde woman's hand resting on her darker companion's forearm. "That's Stanford's brother-in-law, Sinclair Clarke, a panther-shifter. With his wife. She's another Stanford. Sister, I think. I heard she's one powerful witch."

41

"Another witch." Val gave a tiny shake of his head. The sooner he'd be out of here and back home, the better.

"It's a witch town here, bud," the middle-aged man snapped. "Careful what you say."

"Careful?" Mag snorted and drew himself to his full height. "Val's got more magical power than this whole town together."

"Mag." Val quieted his brother with a look. The supernaturals gathered around them were all stronger than most humans. But aside from what looked like a representative from the Daemon World sitting by the back door in medieval-looking regalia, they were all likely much younger than the St-Amands.

And no doubt younger than their own mother, the Ice Witch, born over and over again from an ancient Celtic coven from the old world. While Val had her power within him, and, unlike Mag, had no problem using it, he didn't want to test it here.

Mag was right, they were here to smooth things over, not make new enemies.

"We'll just get a table. Bring us a couple of bottled beers. Something local," Val told the barman. It looked like this evening was a dud. Might as well observe the crowd. "And some water for my dog."

"You got it, boss," the bartender said, obviously not concerned by Sasha's presence in his tavern.

Surveying the various groups as they searched for a seat, scanning for Ren and not finding him, they finally sat down side by side at a table with their back to the main wall.

Mag had returned to studying the female clientele while Val glanced at the Stanford witch and her spouse. She was Diesel's sister. He should really go talk to them.

But Mag was hopeless if left alone. He'd probably hit on someone's girlfriend.

And Val didn't really want to talk to anyone here until he settled things with Stanford. Reassure him that Emme was no issue and that Mag's magical collection was well guarded.

And remind him that while their formidable mom had stayed away from Montreal, she was still alive and well on this continent. The St-Amands could be the warlocks' allies, but they would not do Stanford's bidding.

"Hey, it's her!" Mag elbowed him as the pub's door opened, letting some fresh air in.

"Who?" Val frowned as he continued to scan the room, casting a brief nod at the waitress bringing them their drinks.

"The girl from the shop," Mag explained with eagerness.

Val reluctantly looked to see what made his brother so enthusiastic. The young witch from the craft store stood there, a small figure in an anime logoed T-shirt, plain jeans, and faded sneakers. Her poker-straight black hair fanned against her cheek and down to her chest.

A little geeky, but yes, there was something about her. He felt a kinship in her awkwardness. She, too, didn't seem to want to be there.

She perused the crowd, waved at a few people, before settling her eyes on him.

His breath remained caught in his throat as her gaze of the deepest jade connected with his own. The contact disturbed something in him that had been dormant for centuries.

Seigneur!

The strange force stirring within him had gone straight to his core. His heartbeat pounded madly as a flush of warmth spread down to his groin.

Oh damn. Val instinctively searched for Sasha, who was vigorously lapping water from his bowl at his feet. He couldn't remember ever feeling anything so intense before. He shook himself as he sunk his fingers into the fur of his loyal companion. This could mean trouble.

"I wonder if I should hit on her," Mag was saying.

Val moved his head bleakly as she broke their connection to survey the bar with her head held high before waving with animation at a group of women at the back.

"Sure, why not." He let out a slow exhale, his pulse now steadier, and leaned further back in his chair. He forced himself to look away from her and continue to study the patrons. But he couldn't shake the feeling that this young witch was something else.

And with his entire being, he strongly prayed that Mag would leave this one girl alone.

CHAPTER 3

As soon as the door to the White Reaper had slammed behind her, the loud chatter of patrons above the low track of classic rock had Maisie tightening her jaw with dread.

The roiling in her stomach wouldn't subside. She was not good with crowds. Never had been.

She'd tried the student union at her college in Presque Isle once, forcing an attempt to make friends outside her circle of Berwick Hollow witches and locals, but she'd been dizzied from the overstimulation and never visited again.

If she took a few settling breaths before entering the local pub and sipped on a beer or two during the evening, she could manage. She knew most people here—Conor at the door, Jacob behind the bar, Loni and Hannah serving, and her Uncle Doyle drinking his usual whiskey at the counter. She caught sight of the dark tresses of her cousins, Ava and Marla, at the back.

But this evening was also different. The place was crawling with newcomers for the parley.

There were pockets of people she'd never met before. The middle-aged druids she recognized, but the four stunning girls sitting by the door were new. And she swore the two mysterious women in long flowy summer dresses and multiple necklaces belonged to Esmeralda Devereaux and her Waxing Crescent coven.

And of course, there was them. The two immortals.

As she'd caught the more silent brother studying her, heat had pooled at her center, and she now carefully swallowed to quench the rising flutters in her chest.

Valerian, that was his name, she recalled. Valerian St-Amand. Dark of eyes and luscious curls, with an air of being above them all, seemingly brooding away in equally dark thoughts.

A centuries-old being.

She inhaled sharply as she detected his smallest of nods toward her. *Cripes*, he *did* remember her.

Her heart hammered against her ribcage, and she remained rooted on the spot for a moment.

She shook her head to get out of the trance she seemed to find herself in, having a hard time breaking the powerful eye contact. She wondered if this was what the notorious vampire compelling power was.

Immortal, she corrected herself. They were immortals.

She cast another glance his way and her heart fell to see that he was now in deep conversation with his brother, his brows drawn in a serious frown. He'd already completely forgotten about her.

Shake yourself out of this, Maisie. She made a beeline for the table where Ava and Marla sat with Taylor, another witch from their coven.

Mom was right. She *had* been living a sheltered life. One look from a handsome stranger and she was a mess.

"There you are, coz," Ava called out as Maisie took a seat at her table. "Isn't this wild? All these people."

She shot her cousin a quick smile. "You like this, don't you?"

"You know how I like a change of pace. If it were just up to me, I'd be out of this town in a second."

"It's not up to you, girl." Marla nodded with sympathy as she rearranged the spaghetti strap of her small summer top.

"By the blessed Matronae, no, it's not," Ava said, a grimace appearing on her lips. "Aunty Beaudry would have a fit if I told her I want to leave Berwick Hollow."

"I like it here," Maisie informed them.

"So do I." Taylor brushed a golden curl over her shoulder. She looked delicate tonight in her dusty-pink cotton dress. "We know everyone. It feels safe."

"Exactly." Maisie nodded at the small blonde she'd known since pre-school.

"Oh, I don't know," Marla chimed in. "It'd be nice to live in the city while we're still young enough to enjoy it."

"Nothing to stop you, Mar," Ava said. "Just go get a job there for a while."

Marla leaned forward over the table and picked a handful of bar nuts from the wooden bowl. "Maybe. But I'd miss you all."

"I could go with you," Ava said.

"Ava?" Maisie looked at her, shocked. "But the immortality ritual."

Her cousin was due to enter her undying ceremony soon. Bound to mate to a local male to keep her sanity in check.

"Oh, bloody skull to that," Ava protested. "I don't want to do it."

"You're scared?" Maisie asked.

"No, I'm not scared. But aside from the obvious risks, I don't want to tie myself to someone I'm not truly in love with. Look, I like Jesse, but this is not how I want my life to be."

"Did you tell Aunty Beaudry?" Marla casually popped a peanut into her mouth.

"No. I might just disappear into the night one day." Ava's voice took a wistful tone as she turned to Maisie. "With all that is on *your* plate, we should both make a run for it."

"Coz, hon, you're talking nonsense." Maisie raised a brow. How could her cousin ever think of leaving Berwick Hollow? This was their haven. The only place witches like them felt safe.

"Am I? Have you ever considered that being high priestess of this coven is not the best for you?"

"No. I haven't. It's my duty, Ava." Maisie pressed her lips together, her spine straight, and glanced back at Loni who had just placed a frosty beer mug in front of her.

"She *has* to be HP. We *need* her," Marla said. "I'm a Thibodeau, but I can barely boil water when I seriously put my mind to do magic. And Little Davina is still just a kid."

"I agree," Taylor added. "Aside from you, Ava, Maisie's the strongest one among us all."

"That you are, coz," Ava agreed. "That Holly King enchanted display you created for old Mrs. Sullivan at the bakery last year was something else. She was so upset about not having the energy to decorate for the holidays and there you went with that illusion spell for her. Impressive."

"Oh, my goddesses, so true," Taylor added with appreciation. "Those little figure skaters were doing real twirls and your conjured tiny elves did bake actual holiday cookies. That charm of yours lasted the entire season. It was so clever."

"And that look on Aunty Beaudry when she passed by the bakery and heard *you* did that," Marla chuckled. "That was precious. It was as if she were both proud and annoyed that you could do such beautiful magic."

Taking a quiet sip of her drink, Maisie remembered how grateful Mrs. Sullivan had been for the help. The season's cheer of her shop had always been her pride and joy. Her inability to continue had left her heartbroken. Maisie made herself a mental note to do it for her again this year.

"Regardless of the good you do here, coz, you could still travel," Ava said longingly. "See what's out there. Meet more of our kind."

"Is that what you want to do?" Maisie asked with genuine concern. She had no desire to get to know the Cajun witches any more than necessary, wanting to avoid any possible integration with them since they were known to stir the pot and create trouble.

"Yeah."

"But you can't." Maisie kept her eye contact unwavering to emphasize the weight of their responsibility to their people. Ava would be the one advising her once Aunty Beaudry chose to retire.

"I guess not." Ava shot her a grim smile then turned her gaze to the crowd. "At least we get this right now, all these cool people."

"Did you see the vampires?" Marla said, eyes like saucers in the direction of the St-Amands. "Hot."

"They're immortals," Maisie corrected. "Not vampires." She was a little annoyed that Marla was gawking at them, as if the handsome brothers were hers only.

"What's the difference?" Marla frowned.

"They do have fangs, but they don't feed on human blood like vampires do," Maisie informed her. "They just live an undying life."

"You know about them?" Taylor added.

"My nana just told me what she knows." She purposefully avoided looking in the immortals' direction. She'd learned that not only were they unusually strong, but they also possessed the magic of their mother, the so-called Ice Witch, Charlotte Callan, who was apparently a powerful eclectic sorceress dwelling somewhere secret in North America.

"I heard they can seduce a woman with just one look." Marla stole another glance in the St-Amands' direction. "Just like vampires."

"Nonsense." Maisie snorted despite the strange pull she'd felt at Valerian's gaze.

"They're here because this actual vampire caused mayhem in Seattle. The warlocks didn't know they existed before that," Ava added. "Emmeline Dubois, she's called. And she's his girlfriend, I think."

"Whose girlfriend?" Marla asked. "The one with the dog?"

"Yes," Ava said.

"Pity," Taylor commented. "He's kind of hot with that mysterious look of his."

"I like the one in the leather jacket," Marla chimed in. "He's hella sexy."

"He owns a nightclub in Montreal," Ava informed her, obviously fully versed in the immortal brothers' background.

But Maisie had stopped listening at the mention of a girlfriend. So Valerian St-Amand had a woman in his life. *Emmeline.* Crazy how she found herself suddenly crestfallen. Of course, having lived for centuries, he'd likely had tons of relationships over the years.

She gnawed at her bottom lip and tightened her fist on the handle of her beer mug. The attraction she felt for the stranger was truly immature.

Never mind the immortals, she had a much more

important thing to focus on. She had to pass this bloody test of Aunty Beaudry.

Her stomach suddenly rolled with dread. Would she actually be up to the challenge?

She stared at her cousin Ava who seemed lost in her own thoughts, absentmindedly twirling the straw in her mixed drink while Marla and Taylor continued to gossip about the new people in town.

Ava had the talent. The same if not more than she did. She was right there with her when they defeated the wraiths. And unlike Maisie, she seemed to always have the right spell handy. They came to her naturally, without the hours of studies that Maisie had to put in.

"Ava," she started earnestly, "I know it's not tradition but, do you want it?"

"What?" Ava frowned at her, puzzled at the question.

"The high priestess position. You want to control your destiny." Maisie was fully willing to give it up to help her cousin. "This would be one way."

"High priestess? Me? Are you mad? No, that's your thing." Ava gave her a jaded smile. "It's been like this for generations. I get the unending life and eventually retreat to that eternal meadow Aunty Beaudry always talks about. And you run the show for your mortal life. I'll get to see your great-grandkids grow up."

"Great grandkids?" Maisie cocked a skeptical brow at her cousin. "I don't have much luck with men, so we'll have to count on someone else for Thibodeau descendants. Marla, or Davina."

"Regardless, you're destined to be our HP," Ava assured Maisie with a decisive nod. "Not me."

"You're as gifted a witch as I am," Maisie said. "More even."

"Maybe." Ava shrugged. "But you're the stable one."

"What do you mean?" she inquired.

"You're bound to this place, to this coven. You have no desire to leave."

"That's true. I would die to have to go anywhere else. I love it here. The square with the gazebo in the winter, the color of the foliage in the fall…" She thought of all she loved about her home. "I do draw a big part of my powers from this land."

"I know, coz." Ava tilted her head with empathy. "It's been like this since the first Thibodeau, Beaudry, and Arsenault witches found themselves here after the deportation from Acadia."

"Hundreds of years," Maisie agreed. "I wouldn't want to be away from Berwick Hollow for very long."

"I'd make a terrible HP," Ava added with a grin. "Too lazy. Some magic comes easily to me, so I don't bother learning more. It still wouldn't change the fact that I need to bound myself to Jesse and become immortal."

"Do you love him?" Jesse Sullivan was the local mortal companion Ava had chosen as her anchor to sanity for the immortality ritual. The two would be as good as married in the eye of the coven after the ceremony.

It was what immortal witches had to do to survive the magical toll of the ritual. Aunty Beaudry's own human partner had passed decades ago.

"Oh, I don't know," Ava replied. "I've known him for so long, I don't know anything else."

"I see." Maisie's brows furrowed in concentration as she pondered Ava's fate. To bind yourself to another just to be able to access more powers, she wasn't sure it was a fair trade.

"It'll be okay." Ava shrugged one shoulder and gave Maisie a half-hearted smile.

"I'm sorry, hon."

"Nothing you can do. It is my destiny. Just like you have to follow yours and lead us."

"Right." Maisie inhaled deeply, her mind back on her own predicament. "She's sending me a test, you know. Aunty Beaudry wants to show everyone how gifted I am."

"What?" Marla had tuned in to their conversation. "What test?"

"Some magical trial to convince people I can be high priestess."

"Sorry, but that's dumb," Ava said. "Everyone has seen you fight those wraiths with me. It's known all over the village."

Maisie scanned the crowd, seeing mostly people she didn't know. "She wants me to show *them*."

"Who?" Marla asked. "All of these supernaturals?"

"Yes." Maisie tensed recalling that an attack could come from anywhere at any time. "Or my test could come from one of them."

"Oh, Matronae, who could that be?" Taylor wondered.

Maisie shuddered to think their crone would have her battle one of the daemons. She'd learned they were ruthless. Cripes. She had a sudden, unwelcome thought. It couldn't be one of the immortals now, could it?

"I hope it's not a Waxing Crescent witch," Taylor said. "I heard they fight dirty."

Maisie winced as they all turned to stare at Esmeralda Devereaux's companions by the bar. The alluring witches were laughing loudly at something Uncle Doyle had said, charming the pants off him with their long wavy blonde hair and sun-kissed skin.

"Could be something else," Marla said, "like a tornado or a treacherous hailstorm."

"Or a monster," Taylor said.

"Are you good with monsters?" Ava asked.

"I don't know." She popped the drops of condensation clinging to the outside of her thick glass, her stomach clenching with uncertainty. "I did okay with the wraiths, but I had just reviewed Cousin Jo's Book of Shadows. It's a total fluke that I remembered the spell to dissolve them."

The cousins had cut it close that day. Wraiths were foul and dangerous beings. One touch would be deadly to a witch.

"The worse is that I don't know when it will come." The not knowing was driving her crazy.

"Don't worry about it, coz. It'll come when it comes. You got this." Ava shot her a fast smile and laid a comforting palm on her forearm. "And I'll be right by your side when it happens."

"Thanks."

"My bet is it'll happen tomorrow night during the parley," Marla said. "You know, with everyone there. Full moon and all. The Order of the Black Oak leader is not even here yet."

"Stanford?"

"Yes, my mom heard that his little boy got sick," Marla added. "The kid is better now but Stanford's being delayed. I bet Aunty will want him to see you fight."

"That makes sense." The tension in her body eased. For some strange reason, she thought tonight would be the night. But Marla's theory was more probable. Aunty Beaudry would want the leader who brought them together to witness her abilities.

"About those immortals," Marla winked at them, "aren't they hot?"

Taylor shrugged. "I'd want one of those Seattle huntsmen, myself." She flashed a beaming smile at the hunky males clad in black T-shirts and fatigues sitting at the next table over. "They're human, but oh-so fine."

Finally relaxed, Maisie picked up her beer as Taylor and Marla continued to rank the newcomers' hotness while ogling one after the other.

Maisie was taking a healthy sip of the foamy liquid when the door of the pub burst open.

Ashley Flynn, the gas station attendant, stood wide-eyed at the entrance, her usually well-styled hair a complete mess.

She suddenly let out a scream that chilled the whole place silent.

Flaming hells. Maisie dropped her beer to the table and bolted to her feet, one hand back and ready for a spell.

Ava stood right after her, along with a few others in the bar.

The music stopped as Ashley caught her breath to explain, Conor's arm around her.

"There's a troll," she screeched between ragged inhales as Maisie approached her. "He just threw me out of the station."

Troll. Maisie's brain switched to pure focus as she raced to the entrance.

Super strength, not too smart, usually very hungry. She'd seen a troll once when she was a little girl, but never had to fight it. Her nana had taken care of sending it back where it came from.

"Maisie! Help! He's breaking everything." Ashley grabbed onto both her arms as she pleaded hysterically, her eyes red with tears. "My little Winnie is in her crate in the manager's office at the back. I couldn't get to her."

Maisie heard chairs scrape the floor behind her and loud exchanges from the newcomers, asking what was happening. But she was completely zeroed in on the threat.

The locals were all looking at her now, defaulting to her for leadership since her grandmother wasn't here. Her entire being was on alert, her brain deep in concentration and disconnected from her emotions, bringing back spell after spell in her mind.

"I got this," she told Ashley. Her upper lip was stiff

with resolve as she pushed the tavern's door open. "I'll get her."

"I guess we were wrong." Ava was right beside her as she took off down the street in the direction of the gas station.

"Yep." Her heart racing at the rush of adrenaline pulsing through her veins, she flashed a wary look at her loyal cousin. "This damn test is tonight after all."

CHAPTER 4

"*Seigneur*, bro!" Val had bolted from his chair at the woman's scream. He eyed his brother still lounging back with a perplexed expression on his face, while Sasha nervously hopped on his paws. "A troll?"

A big part of the patrons had rushed outside leaving the place more than half-empty.

"Sounds like they're taking care of it." Mag sampled a sip of his beer before getting on his feet.

"Maisie's going to trash that scum," the middle-aged man at the counter told the barman.

"For sure, Doyle. She will."

Maisie? The girl from the craft shop had barreled outside with her girlfriends and everyone else. Surely, they got this wrong. The town couldn't be relying on that young woman to get rid of an actual troll.

"Mag." Val turned to his brother with urgency. "We've got to help."

"I certainly want to see this." Mag's eyes crinkled with interest. "I'm curious to see what that little witch is going to do against a troll."

"She's just a child," Val protested. Worry for the young woman suddenly grew within him.

"One, she's not a child," Mag countered. "And two, she's got powers, I told you."

"It's a test," one of the waitresses said to them as she walked past to look out the window. "The Beaudry Elder wants Maisie Thibodeau to use her powers in front of everyone."

"Why on earth would they want that?" Val mumbled. This place was insane.

That poor young witch. His own powers twitched as a slew of protective urges rose inside him. He had to help her.

"Come on, Mag." Val snapped his fingers at Sasha and, with his dog at his heels, he followed everyone exiting the bar into the summer air, cheering the young woman on.

Mag was right behind him. They soon found themself in the main square. It appeared as if half of Berwick Hollow was there in a mix of local witches and humans, along with supernaturals here for the parley.

The small gas station stood between two town shops but, unlike their tidy storefronts, the scene there was a complete mess. The small parking lot was littered with spilled washer fluid and shattered glass from the broken window of the convenience store. The sounds of destruction echoed from somewhere inside and a magazine rack suddenly flew out of the front door, landing on the air pump by the curb.

The young witch stood at the front of the crowd alongside the similarly young dark-haired woman who had been sitting with her in the bar. They were both facing the station with grim resolution.

"Who's this with the Thibodeau girl?" Val leaned into the man called Doyle who had walked along with them.

"That's her cousin Ava Beaudry. Those two have been tight since birth. Equally powerful," the man said, his eyes on the brightly lit station. "Ava shouldn't be there. This is Maisie's test. The girl can hold her own. She's as talented as her grandmother."

"The high priestess?" Mag asked.

Val raised a surprised eye to his brother. "You never said she was the high priestess' granddaughter."

"Look!" someone behind them shouted before Mag could explain himself further.

The roof of the small convenience shop had started to shake.

"There it is," a woman screamed.

A large, misshaped head erupted through the front part of the flat rooftop, sending wooden shingles flying everywhere.

The crowd uttered their surprise as the troll burst through, and they all fell back a step.

Soon the beast's whole torso was exposed above the broken roof. The thing was a massive humanoid with a grotesque pug nose and scraggly moss for hair and beard. Its skin was thick bark, his gnarly arms shaped with a complex system of sinuous branches, dotted with tufts of sprouts.

The monster was angrily trashing the place as if throwing a tantrum.

"Good grief!" Doyle yelled. "That Beaudry crone has gone too far."

Val had never seen the likes of it in his entire life.

Fearful for the two young women facing the beast, he raced in closer, pulling on Sasha's collar, Mag dragging himself behind him.

The two barely twenty-something witches stood bravely with their arms steady at their sides, raven hair flowing in the summer wind. Mag had been right, magic hummed from their small-built bodies.

The massive, repulsive troll smashed the facade part of the roof with two giant fists and the whole storefront collapsed, revealing the creature's solid thighs under the moss-like loincloth covering it.

Seigneur, the situation didn't look good. His pulse quickened at the danger the two girls were facing.

"This is messed up, bro." Mag was right beside him, his brows knitted with equal concern as he echoed Val's thoughts out loud.

Val scanned the crowd directly around them. Chelsea Jones held her men at bay and the selkies eyed the troll with distress. The two witches who had sat at the White Reaper's counter were scoping out Maisie and her cousin with derision on their haughty faces. No one seemed ready to do anything.

"We *have* to help," he told his brother.

"No." The dignified older woman from the shop—apparently the coven's high-priestess—had pushed through the front of the group and stared at him with a rigid posture. "This is my granddaughter. She *has* to do this."

"This is not right, Mother." The third woman from the craft store, seemingly Maisie's mom, was white as a sheet, wringing her hands together, her eyes fixed upon her daughter.

"Nonsense, Clara. Maisie is trained." The older woman's tone softened as she wrapped an arm around her daughter and kept her gaze steady at the scene.

"Fight him, Maisie, come on," the blonde who'd been sitting at Maisie's table called out. Confident in her friend's ability, her eyes were bright with excitement as she jumped up and down on her small sandals.

"You cannot interfere in witches' business, immortal."

The high priestess shot him a warning look, the seriousness of her tone unmistakable.

He stared again at the troll who had found the cold food fridges and was popping large tubs of ice cream and soda bottles into his sizable mouth, one after the other, packaging and all.

Val couldn't be the only one here who wanted to help.

"That's one giant troll," a familiar voice sounded in his ear.

Val flinched to find his brother Renaud standing right next to him. In his usual plaid shirt over a white tee, Ren seemed to casually take the whole scene in stride.

"Hey man, you made it." Mag tore his gaze from the impending fight to cast a fond look at their sibling.

"Alcide was called to this conclave," he said, mentioning the alpha of the Domaine-Lassalle wolf pack. "But since you were both coming, he sent me instead to represent the wolf-shifters.

"Glad he did. It's good to see you, bro," Mag said while Val nodded in agreement.

"This is insane, Ren." Magic at his fingertips, fangs ready to tear into flesh, Val eyed the two girls facing the troll, again noticing how fragile they looked in front of all that destruction. "I need to do something."

"Don't." Ren echoed the high priestess's demand. "This is the town's affair. You can't get involved."

With a quiver in his stomach at the danger Maisie faced, Val hesitated. His mind agreed he needed to back off and stay out of it, but his body was ready to swoop in and fight her fight.

Cursing under his breath, he watched her give one squeeze to her cousin's forearm before letting her go.

She advanced toward the huge troll, a lone witch tasked with saving the whole town. Her chin was up, and she was poised for an attack.

No, he just couldn't let this be. His heart raced as if she was his. His entire being was ready to jump at the beast. His fangs were out. His mother's magic hummed inside him.

Ren set a steady palm at his shoulder to stop him from jumping in. Sasha pushed his muzzle at his thigh, and Val rested a hand on his trusty companion's head.

Gritting his teeth in frustration, he forced himself to stand back, and waited for Maisie to cast her first offensive spell.

CHAPTER 5

"*Shyatch mieh!*" Maisie touched her pentacle and erected a protection shield in front of her as she took one step forward to the hulking giant which had managed to take half of the roof off. There was no time to ponder, she had to act and quick.

The monster was now munching on rubber roofing while ransacking the exposed area of the store, not paying any attention to her.

So far, he hadn't reached the back of the gas station where the manager's office was located but it was close. She had to somehow get the huge thing away from there before it found Ashley's dog.

The disgusting creature threw the cash register across the ravaged store and let out a loud belch, its reeking breath making her gag.

How on earth had Aunty Beaudry managed to summon a full-size troll like this? And why had she unleashed it on poor Ashley and her dog? Probably didn't know the tiny chihuahua came to the station on her shifts.

That was the problem with those immortal witches right there, they forgot small details like this. Aunty

Beaudry could rebuild the store back with a few well-chosen spells, but not Ashley's dog.

Breathless with resentment, Maisie took a few more steps forward and strained to hear, hoping the poor thing was not barking too loud.

Thank the Matronae, so far, the chihuahua was still silent.

"Please get my baby," Ashley pleaded behind her. "That horrible thing is going to eat her."

"Honey, be careful," Mom shouted from just a few paces away.

"She's got this, Clara," Nana stated.

And she did. Or at least she had to believe she did. And she had to lure the giant away from the back room.

This was an old-growth forest troll. The telltale bark-like skin, and its limbs shaped of intertwined branches as hard as steel, were unmistakable. She had never encountered one in the flesh but had seen plenty of images. She tried to recall its weaknesses but could only think of its danger. The beast would eat anything in its path, natural and inert material alike, his protruding stomach coated with acidic bile designed to digest anything from animal skin to solid stone.

"I won't let it get to Winnie, Ashley," Maisie promised. She blocked herself from her emotions and worries for the small pooch to focus on saving her. The troll may not get to the little pet but could easily collapse the entire structure and crush the chihuahua under the rumble.

She could use a simple stunning spell, but the beast might keel back over the manager's room. She reviewed her possibilities with analytical detachment. Maybe a mind-control incantation, but those were hard to sustain, and her arm was already killing her from holding up her magical shield.

Her stomach rumbled from the lack of food, and she

wished she had taken the time to eat something today. She could have used the energy.

"They're not super smart, right Ava?" Maisie finally called to her cousin who stood right behind her. She had no problem asking for help if it meant it would beat this monster sooner and faster.

"From what I remember," Ava replied, "not too bright, yes."

"You can't help her, child," Nana warned.

"I can bloody talk to her, can't I?" Ava spat back with spirit. "That poor little doggy!"

She was right. Maisie was willing to take this test but not at the cost of someone's cherished pet.

"If the troll gets anywhere near the back, Ava," she called out, "you jump in and help."

"But Maisie…" her grandmother protested.

"I mean it, Nana. You as well." Aunty could send her another trial. Maisie would not let Winnie get killed for witch politics.

"Very well, Maisie," Nana yielded. "But I still think you can do this by yourself."

"I'll try to get the troll away from the station first," she decided. If the thing was dumb, it might not be too hard. She would send it to the woods, far from the town square, and take it from there.

With one palm up and still holding her protection shield, she found a piece of concrete on the ground from the demolished station and threw it at him. "Hey you! Woodland troll. Down here."

The projectile bounced off the beast's thick bark and it didn't even flinch. *Cripes.*

The creature continued to dig through the wreckage. It fished up a jug of motor oil and swallowed it whole.

Maisie picked another concrete piece and hurled it at him. "Hey troll! Come here."

This time, she managed to hit the back of its head.

The giant stopped and let out a grunt. Its massive hand reached back where the chunk had landed, and the thing slowly turned around with a puzzled look.

The crowd sucked in audible gasps, but she held steady.

"Come this way," she yelled, desperate to get it away from the manager's office.

Keeping her magical shield secure, she threw another slab, this time hitting the troll square in the forehead.

Its scowl deepened as confusion turned to annoyance. The beast picked the broken concrete, which lay at its feet amid popcorn kernels and open snack bags, and chucked it right back in her direction.

The slab bounced off and over her protection shield, avoiding her but landing right in the middle of the crowd. People screamed and spread apart.

Dammit, someone is going to get hurt.

"*Seigneur,* brother." The deep voice reached her ears, sending warm chills to her spine. "She can't defeat this alone."

But she had to. And she could. She just had to let the troll focus on her first and away from the gas station. With her entire being fixated on her purpose, she stood her ground as the troll straightened its spine up to its full height.

Flaming hells. The creature's wide and flaccid body towered above her like a gigantic menacing living tree.

She swallowed and endeavored to keep her mounting fear at bay.

Too many people stood around watching the monster with a mix of shock and awe. "Stay back!" she ordered. She couldn't afford to be distracted with protecting them, too.

"*Shyatch mieh, Matronae.*" She implored the triple deities

to protect her as she continued to keep her shield firmly in place. Her other palm was at her thigh and ready to strike forward at the right moment.

"Come get me, you big ugly brute." She had no idea if the troll understood her language but yelling at him made her feel better as she expelled some of her drummed-up nervous energy. "Come on!"

The troll took a few more steps in her direction and away from the back room, shedding parts of the crumbled building as it ambled forward.

There, that's it.

But luck was not on her side.

A tiny bark erupted from the station. *Dammit. Winnie!*

Now that she had started to yap, the dog wouldn't stop. Her high pitch whine echoed noisily in the air.

The troll had heard it, too. The creature stopped and turned back. Its misshapen head tilted to the side with curiosity.

"Hey, here!" Maisie yelled at it and threw another slab of concrete. But the giant didn't even register.

It took a step in the direction of the yapping, smashing parts of the roof as it moved. So far, the only last third of the building remained.

Oh shit. Her plan wouldn't work.

"Anyenthex!" She dropped her shield. Both palms thrust forward and she slammed the troll with a powerful magical blast.

The hit knocked the beast back in a bright flash of bluish glow.

The crowd behind her gasped while someone beside her cheered.

But she watched in horror as her magic spread along its bark-like skin in a subdued glimmer and slowly dissolved in the beast's thick hide.

"It's no good, coz!" Ava shouted. "These kinds are immune to offensive spells. Their bark absorbs all of it."

"Now you tell me," Maisie grumbled under her breath.

She should have known this. She was being tested to show she would be a good high priestess and right now she was failing the most basic skill. *Dammit.*

Her spell might not have knocked it out, but the troll didn't look too happy. The creature turned an angry look at her over his shoulder, picked up what looked like his sturdy wooden club, and trod out of the shambles to face her fully.

Oh hells! Things were about to get real. Adrenaline rushed through her veins and all the way to the back of her spine.

She no longer cared about showing off.

Forget this whole public trial. She was witch enough to be accepted by strangers.

Her only goal was to save Ashley's dog. The poor thing was still yapping loudly with fear, just on the other side of the troll. She had no choice but to ask for help, test be damned to the seven hells.

"Ava, get the dog," she ordered. "I'll distract the troll."

Her cousin nodded and ran to the alley beside the destroyed building while Maisie picked up another lump of concrete to throw at her foe.

"Take that, woodland creep!" she shouted as the concrete chunk nicked its bulbous nose.

The troll snorted. It shook its head a few times and lifted its huge club overhead, growling with rage. It smashed its bludgeon to the blacktop at its feet.

Maisie recoiled as the ground shook. Her adversary now focused its entire attention her way, no longer caring about the yappy dog.

She held her breath as Ava blasted the back door of the station in a flare of bright magical light before running into what was left of the building. Her cousin soon came back carrying Winnie in her small crate, a protective shield above both of them.

She jogged back to pass the cage to Ashley who swooned with gratefulness. Soon the chihuahua was in Ashley's arms, lapping her face with relief.

"Come on, everyone," Maisie ordered between clenched teeth. "Get away from here."

But the crowd just wanted to see what she would do.

"Blast him again, Maisie," someone called out.

"Yeah," Marla yelled. "Just fry him with an electric flash!"

Maisie ignored the useless advice to refocus on her enemy. With Winnie out of the way, she could work more clearly. If her opponent wasn't going to be affected by magic, she had to somehow get him out of town.

The troll advanced forward and once more cracked his huge club upon the ground. The gas station's metal sign shook above her as she jumped sideways right before the sign broke from the vibration and crashed where she was standing.

Sweat beaded upon her forehead as her heart hammered heavily against her ribcage. This was *not* easy. She held on tight to her protective shield. She could try distracting it.

"*Saothrechl meilludh…*" She intoned the start of an illusion spell. "*Saothrechl!*"

Concentrating on the image in her mind and calling forth the magical energy inside her, she fashioned a large glowing eagle in the sky. She compelled the wide radiant wings of her mystical bird of prey to slowly flap right under the troll's nose as her creation hovered elegantly in the air.

"Go after it, troll!" Maisie shouted. "Go."

If she could get the giant to chase after her trickery, she'd get the beast out of town and into the woods.

The troll froze and stared at the majestic raptor with fascination as the animal gently soared away toward the forest before looping back for another tease.

The monster swiped at it and, annoyed to discover it was just an illusion, turned what looked like a sharp eye down at her.

Cripes. The brute didn't seem fooled at all by her magic. Not as dumb as she'd originally believed.

The beast planted both gnarly feet in front of her, and again smashed his club at its feet with defiance. Her magical bird dissolved as she shuddered with alarm.

Her foe opened its ugly mouth and roared, revealing rotten stumpy teeth and a disgusting mossy tongue. Dribbles of milky-white fluid sloshed over the pavement, burning a deep hole right in front of her.

Shit. Lightheaded with dread, she readjusted her stance at the gruesome sight.

A line from Cousin Jo's bestiary in the White Holly Book of Shadows hit her. This whitish sap-like retch was so acidic, it would burn her to death. She had to find a way to overthrow this bully. Now!

Damn. Think Maisie, think.

But she had no time to think. The troll slammed his club down once more, the air current it created swishing her hair. She barely managed to avoid it with a quick sidestep.

Holding her breath, she took off into a sprint and scurried right between its colossal legs before it could raise the weapon up again.

The troll looked down at its feet, puzzled not to find her. She realized her mistake, trapping herself in the middle of the parking lot with the destroyed station behind her.

If she could maybe figure out what the troll wanted, she would have something to work with. But no, the beast desired nothing, it was just mad as hell that she'd interrupted its dinner.

He grunted again as he looked over its shoulder and found her. A deadly chill ran down her spine as she caught its look of pure hatred.

She gulped with fear—holding with all she had onto her defense shield—as it marched again toward her. The thump of its club underscored each of its angry steps, a roll of its massive shoulders displaying its show of strength. If one of those blows fell down on her head, her protection sphere would barely hold.

She surveyed her surroundings for something to defend herself. Break the station's sign pole and levitate it on its head, maybe? She'd need to drop the shield and there was no guarantee the monster could get knocked unconscious with something that small compared to its massive size.

Her gaze fell on the crowd in the town square behind the troll. She caught sight of Mom wringing her hands and Ava's tight lips. She could call on Nana but that would be admitting failure.

Those two Cajun witches would report back to Esmeralda and the Louisiana coven would make their move on her people.

Her pulse pounding against her ribcage, she walked backward a few more paces until she backed into a gas pump. Damn, trapped.

Her brain wildly flipped to everything she knew, every piece of fact she had studied. Her arm heavy and sore from bearing the protective spell, she searched the troll's face, willing something helpful to come to her. Its eyes burned with raw anger hellbent on smashing her.

The rubber hose pushed into her back when it suddenly hit her. *Fire!*

Trolls were not immune to fire.

Yes! That's it! She held the shield up as she rummaged in her jeans pocket for her credit card at the back of her cell phone. The troll had stopped and was now considering her with a dangerous flare of its nostrils.

Come on, Maisie. Come on!

With one hand, she got the card into the slot and pushed in her passcode. The troll snarled as she pressed the large button for the fuel selection, her pulse mad with adrenaline.

"Maisie, watch out!" Ava shouted.

She was clasping the gas nozzle in one hand when the giant struck its club into her protection sphere. The blow reverberated into her arm and nearly toppled her to the ground.

"Shyatch mieh, Matronae." Maisie called for more protection, keeping her shield firm. The spell was barely holding on and she was weakening. She silently prayed to her deities for her plan to work.

She needed her energy for one last spell. With both legs firmly anchored to the ground and the hose stretched as far in front of her as it would go, she pumped gas in the troll's direction, using her magic to direct the liquid away from her.

The fuel left a stream upon the ground to pool around the beast's stumpy feet.

The club came down once more but this time she was ready. She dropped the gas nozzle to the ground and jumped back to the concrete ledge surrounding the gas tanks to avoid the strike.

She released her shield and shoved both palms forward in one mighty swoop.

"Strieahadhr!" she roared.

The fuel ignited at once under her spell, flames licked at the troll's feet. The beast tumbled backward at the burn and toppled on the flaming concrete. The monster howled in pain, rolling back and forth into the fire, coating its thick bark with the blazing gas, which, igniting, weakened its natural shield.

This was her chance.

"*Stryos!*" She hit the giant square in the chest with her most powerful stunning spell.

The troll fell back unconscious on the pavement, its tongue hanging out at one side.

The whole crowd clapped as she finally took in a breath. She had done it. Passed Aunty Beaudry's test. She had vanquished the troll all by herself in front of the supernatural community.

Tears welled behind her eyelids at the sudden release of tension. She bent forward to catch her breath, her palms clammy with sweat. Her heartbeat started to regulate again. Flaming hells, that had been close.

But she had succeeded. A small, satisfied smile appeared on her lips.

Feeling in complete control and keenly aware of the approving look of the crowd upon her, she walked closer to the troll, dousing the fire with one quiet splay of her hand before turning back to her group of supporters where Mom was looking at her with obvious relief.

"I've passed your test, Aunty Beaudry," she shouted out in the evening air, not seeing the crone among the cheering assembly.

The old witch had to be somewhere, watching. Maisie was still angry that little Winnie had been caught in the crossfire.

"So you have, Maisie." Her nana was blinking with pride. "Well done! No one will question you now. Our future High Priestess of the White Holly."

"Oh my gods, watch out!" someone suddenly yelled from the crowd.

Maisie barely caught Ava's fearful wide-eyed stare before a potent belch echoed behind her.

She had no time to turn around before being scooped off her feet by a pair of powerful arms and tumbled back onto the pavement.

What in the Matronae…

A commanding male voice snapped loudly in the night. "*Vahrasth hyenthx!*"

Valerian St-Amand had his arm around her waist, his strapping body solid against hers. His fangs were out, his handsome features twisted gaunt.

Stunned, she watched the troll now conscious and back on its knees, surrounded by the large pool of caustic milky sap he had just retched. The nauseating liquid was burning straight through the blacktop where she had stood just a moment ago.

Had it not been for the immortal holding her tight against his sturdy chest, she would be scorching in agony.

She could barely ponder the wonderful sensation of his strong arms on her weak body and his enticing scent folding over her, before he let out an unyielding mystical command.

"*Satirsth!*"

At that one word, a bright blast of energy shot out from St-Amand's palm and with magic she'd never experienced before, he blasted the troll dead on its knees.

CHAPTER 6

"Oh shit, bro." Ren shot Val a stark expression. "You shouldn't have done that."

Val let the witch go at once and she toppled on her feet. Her puzzled, captivating gaze of deep jade drummed a beat upon his soul. He was flushed with desire at the sight of a lock of her dark hair caught against the bottom of her shapely lips.

He wanted to say something to her, but her family had already crowded around her, inquiring about her well-being in a dissonance of worried shrieks and stern warnings.

It had only been for an instant, but he recalled how her heart had beat like crazy against his chest as she caught her breath. Her strong but supple body pressed against him, and her fresh scent stirred strange feelings inside him.

A flush of warmth hit him straight below the belt.

Seigneur! He was dying for more. What was wrong with him?

The people in the square were commenting loudly to each other about the fight they'd just witnessed while Mag shook his head at him, his lips curling with amusement.

His magic receded along with the glow of his mother's magical sigil at his wrist. He raised a slow brow at his brother Ren who still considered him with a condemning gaze, his brows knitted together.

"Like hell," Val replied with a deadly look. He wouldn't stand back and let the woman be burnt by the bile of this foul creature. "She could have been killed."

"Dammit, coz! That was freakin' scary!" The witch who had saved the dog was shouting among the small crowd surrounding Maisie, while the mother rearranged her daughter's disheveled hair.

Maisie cast one look at Val over her shoulder, her gaze filled with something he couldn't quite read, before she was again swarmed by her family.

Val scratched Sasha's head as his pet leaned his heavy body against his leg. He was thankful to see the young woman unharmed, but he couldn't ignore the inexplicable trickle of sadness that had touched his heart at releasing her from his embrace.

Why should she affect him? She was just another woman, talented for sure, but nothing to him.

"You're such a dumbass." Ren slapped a resigned palm at his back. "Always the savior."

"Told you she was attractive," Mag teased. "She's all yours, man."

"Uhm." Val gazed upward with annoyance as he repressed his emerging feelings. Aside from his string of faithful dogs over the centuries, there was no place for any sort of attachment in his life. The sooner he would be out of this senseless town, the better.

"St-Amand of Mont-Royal!" A creaky but harsh voice cut through the crowd.

He turned to see who had heckled him and his gaze rested on a short elderly lady in long black skirts and a fringed paisley shawl. Her frizzy gray hair was tied in an austere bun at the back of her head. She was eying him with a belligerent look on her heavily-lined features.

"Who do you think you are," she scolded, "messing with my witches like that?"

"Oh, bloody skull, Great-Aunty, he saved Maisie," the witch called Ava replied before looking down at the corpse of the fallen being he'd slayed. "And what in the seven hells is that wicked beast you summoned? Was that even real?"

"It was a troll, girl. A simple old-growth forest troll illusion that I fashioned myself." She waved her arm around in a flurry of silky tassels and the giant and its bile dissolved into the pavement, leaving nothing behind. "A fine test for your cousin."

"That's messed up, Aunty." Ava sneered, but Maisie stared anxiously at the crone.

"Messed up? No, it was perfect," the elder asserted with her head held high before pointing an accusatory finger back at Val. "And you! *You* were wrong to help Maisie like that. This was *her* test."

"Agatha," the high priestess chimed in, her hand calmly resting on the pearls at her neck. "That's a bit harsh, don't you think?"

Val regarded them all, one witch after the other. He ended by laying his eyes on Maisie, her pretty face now pinched with resentment.

"What are you all staring at?" The old witch ignored High Priestess Thibodeau to turn a defiant look at the people listening in from the town square. She kept her lips pursed and her frail shoulders back, unmistakable mystical energy radiating from her stooped frame.

"She almost died, Agatha. You nearly killed my daughter." Indignant, Maisie's mother shielded her offspring with her body, oblivious to the fact that said daughter had brought a full-size troll to its knees with some powerful magic and cleverness.

Meanwhile Maisie remained quiet, but her fists were balled with agitation. Val had a quick wish to take her away from all the drama and let her recover from her ordeal in peace.

"Clara, *chère*, it had to be done," the elder continued. "Your daughter needs to prove herself before taking over after your mother."

Val exchanged a quiet look with his brothers and saw Mag give him a soundless shrug while Ren silently advised him to add nothing to the witches' mayhem.

"You put Winnie at risk, Aunty." Maisie gently pushed her mother to the side. Her tone was filled with hostility. "Ashley's dog could have been crushed or eaten alive."

"How was I supposed to know Ashley brings her pet to work?" The old woman shrugged. "And you saved the puny thing, didn't you? Or I should say, Ava saved her."

Maisie looked furious now, her face taking a reddish tint. She closed the distance between her and the older witch. The air around them electrified with sparks of uncontained magical energy.

"You put a poor little creature at risk just so you could show off to outsiders, possibly hurt one of them in the crossfire," Maisie fumed. "Don't you ever think about anything beyond politics?"

"I have to, child. I have to," the old woman replied with a bitter twist of her mouth. "Who else will? Certainly not your grandmother." She looked at the crowd of supernaturals who had started to disperse in the direction of the White Reaper, before turning her irritated gaze to the high priestess.

"*This* would never have to happen if you hadn't sold us to the Order of the Black Oak, Marianne. This parley is an abomination." She was incensed now, no longer interested in Maisie but raging at her grandmother. "Old Marie-Aimée Thibodeau and Angélique Beaudry—may the Matronae bless their souls—would turn in their graves to know you are allying us with others."

"We are older than these warlocks," she continued. Her lips curled back with hostility, the fury rolling off her felt by everyone. "And what about these other creatures, selkies, daemons, and worse? We were doing fine on our own."

"The world is changing, Aunty Beaudry." Maisie's tone had become calm, her keen intelligence noticeable as she added, "Everyone is more and more connected. It's only a matter of time before our village is known to strangers. Nana is right. We need alliances."

Aunty Beaudry. Val finally recognized the last name. So, this was Agatha Beaudry, the immortal crone who looked after this coven. She had a strange way of showing her protection with nearly killing one of her own tonight.

The old woman huffed and, unconvinced by Maisie's sensible explanation, turned the full of her anger in Val's direction.

"And you." She again pointed at him and his brothers, raising her tone to a shrill, "Vampires. How dare you get involved, boy."

Mag snickered beside Val while Ren crossed his arms and leaned back on his heels to consider the woman from his full height.

Val took a deep breath. They were here to make alliances, like Maisie had said. Not cause more trouble.

"*Madame.*" Val nodded at the elder and extended a hand, trying his best to contain his annoyance at the old witch under a veneer of formality. "I am Valerian Callan St-Amand, Mount-Royal Immortal. And here are my brothers Magnovald and Renaud. We are the sons of Charlotte Callan, Ice Witch of the Celtic Isles. We come here at the bequest of Diesel Stanford."

The Beaudry woman pursed her lips and hurled a dark

look in the direction of Maisie's family who was now moving away from the scene. Maisie's mother was dragging her daughter with hushed tones, while Ava shook her head with displeasure as she followed them.

His senses dulled to see the back of Maisie's head as she was being carried along with them, her black hair floating in the dark.

She cast him a quick look over her shoulder and his heart skipped a beat at the short but intense connection. She bit her lip before turning away from him as her mom pulled her by the shoulders. Soon they were taking off in the direction of the Crafty Sprite shop.

"She failed the test," Agatha Beaudry was now grumbling. "And it's all your fault."

"Failed?" Ren asked.

"*Sacrament*," Mag added. "What are you talking about, woman. That little witch took down your disgusting troll all by herself. Very cunningly, at that."

"*He* saved her." Her finger crooked toward Val once more as the frown between her eyes deepened.

"You don't like us much, do you," Ren noticed.

"It's your father I don't like," she groused.

"Our Father? You knew our Papa Antoine?" Mag inquired with surprise. "Are you as old as we are?"

Val remained silent still watching the young witch he had just saved. Her silhouette in the midst of her family was getting smaller and smaller under the nearly full moon. With somberness, he patted Sasha, now quietly sitting at his side.

"She means the other father," Ren spat.

Again, Val redirected his attention to the Beaudry elder and his brothers discussing their lineage. What did this old battle-ax know of their birth father? Nothing, he was sure. Mom had never, ever talked of the mysterious Ambrus the Exiled.

In three hundred years of existence, none of them had ever met him. Ren had made it clear he wanted nothing to do with him while their brother Griffon had been searching the world over for him for the better part of the last century. Val was much too busy with Emme's cursed vampires to worry about some creature that had never bothered finding them.

As far as Val was concerned, Antoine St-Amand was his father. A mere mortal, perhaps, but Papa had supported and loved their mother despite knowing what she was. A quiet and just man, he had been the best father anyone could ever wish for.

His chest tightened with guilt. Not being by Papa's bedside at his death remained, to this day, one of Val's biggest regrets.

"That foreign immortal is not really our father," he informed the old witch, his tone cool.

"You're the sons of a legendary sorceress, I grant you that," the old woman conceded. "But you," her gnarled finger rose up in front of her again, "you shouldn't have gotten involved in Maisie's trial."

"Didn't you see the fight?" Val narrowed his eyes at her as Sasha pressed his body against him, sensing the woman's anger. "She would have been burnt from the troll's corroding bile had I not jumped in to help."

"And so what?" she said flippantly. "There are risks involved to anyone who wants to lead."

"You would have let a young witch of your own coven be disfigured just to prove her worth?" Val couldn't believe it. *What a wicked shrew!*

"What I do in my coven is no business of yours, St-Amand," the Beaudry Elder argued. "Hadn't your mother taught you of our ways?"

The truth was that their mother had taught them very little. He knew she was not just immortal, but reborn a few generations over from an ancient Celtic coven of sorcer-esses before she had finally settled into her current persona of the Ice Witch. But aside for training them in the craft when they were children—the power drawn from her mark which they all donned on their wrists—she had barely mentioned her connection to the witches of the New World.

He'd had an awkward reunion with her a good fifty years after Justin had found his coffin under the mountain. And then just a few calls to check in along the years.

"Our mother is irrelevant here," Val spat with a tight upper lip. "I would not stand by and let a girl be burned by acid just to protect your politics."

But the witch had lost interest in the conversation. Instead, she seemed to be mulling things over, her outrage suddenly deflated. "How will we convince everyone that Maisie can ascend to the High-Priestesshood now that she failed to save herself?"

"You truly want her as your high priestess?" Val wondered. "She's still quite young."

"She's twenty-five," the crone said. "Don't be fooled by her appearance. You saw her, the girl *is* a force of nature."

Val was taken aback by the sense of pride in the old woman's tone. The crone had been sabotaging Maisie with a very dangerous test.

"She would have shielded herself from that caustic upchuck," the crone added. "I have no doubt about it. I just needed everyone here to see it. The bloody Waxing Crescent witches were right there, and don't forget the banshees. Those Davenport freaks have always looked down upon us."

"I don't deny that she's truly something." He recalled her presence of mind at pumping gas on the ground. "The fire was very clever."

"The girl has always been like this. All intellect," the

Beaudry Elder explained. "A bit awkward with people though, which is why she needed this test in front of everyone this one time and be done with it."

"We can vouch for her at the parley, if it's any help," he suggested. He had no idea what possessed him but here he was offering to take the witches' side because of some strange emotions brought in by being around the Thibodeau witch for a brief moment.

"You?" Agatha Beaudry stared at him, temporarily shaken.

"Val?" Mag broke his silence.

"Well, why not?" Val glanced at Ren who just shrugged at him.

"Huh…" A shrewd expression crossed the old witch's eyes. "An alliance between the White Holly Witches and the Mount-Royal Immortals. I wonder what bloody Diesel Stanford would say about that?"

"Someone looking for me?" The deep tone cutting through the summer night took everyone by surprise.

Val slowly turned to the newcomer. So this was Diesel Stanford.

The warlock leader stood alone in the middle of the deserted street, his casual white T-shirt under a long black duster, dirty-blond hair falling over one eye.

"You're Stanford?" Mag was as frigid as their own city on a winter day.

"And you three are St-Amand brothers?" Diesel swaggered leisurely toward them, dropping a steel-blue gaze at the small crowd still left in the square. He turned back to the brothers and the Beaudry elder. "I thought there were six."

Val strode ahead past the crone to examine Stanford up close, his siblings lining up at each side of him, Sasha at their heels.

Ren had remained silent, but Val could feel the readiness to attack rushing through his sibling's veins. His brother was not just here as a spokesperson for Alcide Gauthier, alpha of the wolf pack dwelling in the Domaine-Lassalle mountains just outside their city. He was also representing the Montreal immortals. Ren took his status as protector very seriously.

"They couldn't make it," Val curtly told Stanford.

"A shame." The warlock's features remained unreadable, but the magical power humming in him was evident. This was someone not to cross unless absolutely necessary. "So, what's all this? I passed a group of locals in the street talking about a fight."

"Nothing to concern you, Stanford," the Beaudry elder said. "Just witches and immortals' business."

The sorcerer leader's expression eased but the self-assurance remained, palpable behind his relaxed façade. "Witches and immortals' business are *my* business now."

Defiance rose within Val. If Mag hadn't let Emme access his magical artifact, the Order of the Black Oak would have left them alone.

Conflicted, he mused that while Diesel Stanford was much younger than they were, he was likely equally matched in magic to himself and his brother Griffon. Mag and the others barely used their abilities. And the warlocks had powerful allies, especially with Malcolm being King of the Daemon World.

Val suddenly wished Justin were here instead of them. As a scholar, he would have known how to handle this better. Val wanted to collaborate, but he didn't want their family under the warlocks' thumb, either.

And here, swayed by feelings he shouldn't entertain, he had just offered an alliance with the White Holly witches.

"The parley is not until tomorrow," he finally replied. Not giving any hint of the tension in his limbs at the thought of being under anyone's control, he kept his gaze casual. "I guess we'll see exactly how deeply we're willing to go to entangle ourselves in your world."

On these words, he slowly turned away from Stanford and the Elder Beaudry to stride down the dark, empty street along with his brothers, Sasha padding beside him.

They were St-Amands, dammit. Living on their own terms for centuries.

He was not about to let some other supernatural—not even the small but powerful witch who had stirred something inside him—change any of their involvement with others.

CHAPTER 7

*M*aisie tugged nervously at her new floor-
length ivory dress. She stood with Ava and a
few other witches right behind Nana and Aunty Beaudry
under the canopy of majestic blooming white holly trees in
the sacred clearing of the Berwick Hollow woods. The two
White Holly elders sat in the restorative circle, along with
the other supernatural leaders summoned by Diesel Stanford of the Order of the Black Oak.

Some of them, she did not know. But she could now
identify the old banshee sisters, April and June Davenport,
as well as Esmeralda Devereaux, dressed in flowy chiffon
of many bright colors, with her equally flashy coven
members standing behind her, and old bearded Christopher Lewis from the Greystone druids.

And of course, there were the St-Amands. Her heart
fluttered just to look at Valerian, sitting tall with his beautiful dog by his chair, his brothers flanking him.

The summertime breeze was gentle under the full
moon. They had brought summer wine to their guests and
after the traditional sharing of cakes, the supernatural
heads had conferred.

There had been talk of a rising evil on the west coast whom one of the leaders, a menacing-looking warlock with long hair partly held back with a leather cord, had assured was contained. And a mention of a rogue witch from Seaport who was still on the run.

Maisie listened carefully, taking in the abrasive voice of Aunty Beaudry and the more conciliatory tone of her grandmother. The elders both wanted her to take Nana's place, but would Maisie ever be able to do so?

As she heard their high priestess giving in to the outsiders a little by agreeing to loosen the borders of the town, while maintaining strong boundaries for their coven, she wondered if she would ever strike that deliberate mindset and protect their own in the role of high priestess.

And that, of course, could only happen if the new council about to form would get behind her leadership.

Nana had heard from Aunty Beaudry that the Mount-Royal Immortals were ready to back her. She gulped as she studied the darkly handsome man right across from them in the sacred circle. His hand rested upon his dog's neck, and she recalled his strong grip around her waist.

She caught his gaze as a summer eve's breeze brushed against her, her gauzy dress fluttering around her legs. Heat flushed to her chest, and she licked her lips at the intensity of his stare.

Just last night, she'd been seconds from agonizing disfigurement, possibly death, but he had swooped in and with one word had destroyed her foe.

Satirsth. The spell was an old one. She recognized it from Cousin Jo's Book of Shadows. A spell from a tradition that existed well before her own, which could only be traced back to the 1500s. His was an ancient magic that came from the witch her ancestors called la *Sorcière du Clan de Callan.*

No one here practiced this kind of sorcery.

He got it from his mother, Aunty had said. *I had no idea she had passed it to her sons.*

And he had saved her with it.

She'd been so distracted by the relief of finally vanquishing the troll, and rattled by the spectators, that she'd underestimated her enemy.

But he had been there and scooped her to safety.

"I can promise you all that Emmeline will be contained," Valerian was now saying. "She'd never left Montreal before this, and Dunsmuir, here, has made sure she won't."

The ominous warlock Malcolm Dunsmuir, King of the Daemon World, nodded in agreement.

"What will you do, chain her to the basement?" April Davenport called out with hostility, taking a drag from her long cigarette holder. "You're talking about my great-niece Elsa's life here."

Maisie had just learned the whole reason for the presence of the St-Amand brothers from Aunty Beaudry who had dropped by the Crafty Sprite to confer with the other witches right after her trial. Mag was known to collect magical artifacts, and something called the Impervious Stone had found its way into the hands of Emmeline Dubois, immortal companion—or perhaps even girlfriend —of Valerian St-Amand.

She had given the pendant, which allowed the wearer to be invulnerable to any mystical ward, to a cursed vampire youth named Evan Grant. He had used the artifact to get into the Davenport's house in the Pacific Northwest and attack their great-niece, an infant banshee. They had believed that drinking from the supernatural baby would free them from their constant hunger for human blood. Valerian had then raced to Seattle, befriended Dunsmuir, and brought Emmeline and Evan back to Montreal.

"The Grant kid is indeed chained in my basement." Valerian's tone held a glacial undercurrent. "He's being reformed and taught how to survive as a vampire without hurting others. My brother Magnovald will be responsible for him when he's weaned. Emmeline remains with my Nostredame Disciple and me at the *Sanctuaire des Truands*."

Maisie straightened her spine to fight the turmoil in her heart at hearing that Valerian and this Emmeline lived under the same roof.

"I say you should have killed them both," April Davenport spat back at the immortal. "Malcolm?"

"No," Dunsmuir said, his dark gaze betraying his half-daemon essence. "Evan is family."

Maisie recalled Aunty Beaudry had mentioned that Evan was actually the brother of Dunsmuir's wife who ruled as Queen of the Daemon World. It all seemed so complicated.

"Enough," Diesel Stanford ordered. "We are not rewriting the past. We have all agreed here to co-exist in peace while informing each other of any crisis in our worlds. Now that the Mount-Royal Immortals are known to us, I put my trust in them to abide by these accords."

"And what of the artifacts?" June Davenport, the tiny banshee sitting next to her more imposing sister, asked in a determined voice.

"Yes, the artifacts." April Davenport blew out cigarette smoke into the air. "They can't keep them."

"Val?" Mag shot them all a feral smile as he slouched back in his seat with defiance.

Valerian cast him a quieting look before addressing the circle. "My brother has as much right as you all have to own as many artifacts as he wishes," he proclaimed.

"But how do we know they will not be used for evil?" the druid shouted.

"Yeah, you're no warlocks," Esmeralda Devereaux trumpeted.

"No. We are not." Mag suddenly stood from his chair, a formidable adversary with his dark curls, commanding posture, and leather motorcycle jacket. "But we have been on this land before any of you have. And I will bloody do whatever I want when it comes to magic."

Maisie's heart sped up at witnessing his outburst. The charmer was gone, the predator in him fully in the open.

Ava gripped her wrist. "Damn, coz," she whispered.

A chill ran up her spine at the obvious hostility in the air. The tension was so dense she could no longer take it. His brother had saved her life. She had to do something.

Maisie stepped forward by her grandmother's side. "He's right!"

Apprehensive about overstepping her position, her hands shook but her spirit was filled with righteousness.

"His family has been here since the crossing of their mother in 1669." She had spent the night researching the St-Amands' history and knew her facts. "They have as much rights as we witches of the White Holly have," she added, "landing in Acadia the same century. And certainly, as much as the Order who was founded a whole hundred years later when the Seaport warlocks received their magic under a black oak tree from a mysterious sorceress."

Maisie had everyone's attention now. She winced. Her discourse was for sure no way as sleek as her grandmother's measured speeches.

Valerian offered a warm smile in approval of her defense, and she swallowed hard. *Now what?*

Diesel Stanford tilted his head in her direction. "And who might you be?"

"My name is Maisie Thibodeau. Witch of the White Holly." Channeling her ancestry, she put as much confidence in her words as she could. She felt Ava's palm on her back as she held her breath.

"One of yours, Marianne?"

"My granddaughter. Future high priestess of our coven." Nana regally scanned the circle, daring anyone to contradict her.

"Ah." Stanford presented Maisie with a benevolent smile. He raked back the dirty-blond curl that had fallen over his eye. "I heard you took down a massive troll last night, all by yourself."

She nodded quietly, feeling the weight of everyone's gaze on her.

"Maisie is powerful and ready to take on the leadership after her grandmother." Aunty Beaudry held her gray head high. After all the bickering, the elder was now standing up for her.

"She didn't do this alone. The immortal here helped her." Esmeralda's disdain was palpable. "Your small coven is no longer strong enough to stand on its own, Agatha. You need to join our rank."

"Join your ranks?" Aunty Beaudry sneered. "And who, pray tell, will lead us? You?"

"Yes, me."

"Never." Aunty Beaudry's nostrils flared as she stared Esmeralda down while Nana let out a slow, controlled breath trying to keep her cool. "Maisie is witch enough for you all."

"But she did have help last night," June Davenport said. "I saw it, too. We all did. If it weren't for St-Amand, she'd be dead. Or disfigured beyond recognition."

Maisie noticed Aunty's fists tightening, her knuckles turning white. The crone had been ranting all night about the St-Amands' involvement in her trial. But had ended the night pleased that they wanted to support her and ally themselves with the White Holly witches.

That mother of theirs was an impressive sorceress. Having the sons on their side was a feat Esmeralda could not beat.

"I don't know, Esme." One of the copper-haired beauties that Maisie had identified as Maritimes selkies suddenly spoke. She was older than her companions but still possessed an aura of serenity that enhanced the charm of her handsome features. "The young Thibodeau was astonishing last night. That charmed eagle, such beautiful magic."

"I agree." Chelsea Jones, sitting primly in her business suit, nodded firmly at Diesel. "The witch showed some clever thinking on the spot. She certainly impressed me."

Maisie warmed at the compliment. The Seattle woman led a team of fearless supernatural hunters, and her appreciation was something of which to be proud.

"She's too young," the Greystone druid leader huffed. "She needs more training, more tests."

Maisie racked her brain on how to prove herself to help her coven.

"The test last night was fine," her mother asserted. "She doesn't need more."

"We will test her!" Esmeralda declared. "It's obvious you're getting soft in your middle age, Marianne."

"Soft!" Ava burst out. "Maisie nearly died last night."

"And that's exactly my point, young woman." The Cajun witch smirked at Ava with a superior look on her perfectly made-up features. "She's not strong enough."

"I'll take your trials," Maisie suddenly barked at Esmeralda. She was determined to prove herself worthy to her detractors. "Once these accords are done, I will come south and take all the tests you want me to take."

Everyone was looking at her again. Oh, flaming hells, what had she just agreed to?

A wave of respect rippled through the crowd. But the White Holly witches didn't feel the same.

"Are you crazy, coz?" Ava griped. "They won't leave you alive."

Mom had turned a pained look upon her. She knew they would not treat her kindly, that she could likely die in any of their so-called trials.

"I may have a better solution." Stanford's voice cut straight through the chitchat, his very essence humming with contained power and even temper, reminding everyone that he was their leader.

"Solution?" Mom asked cautiously.

"You Davenports and Waning Crescent witches want this young woman to prove her worth."

"The druids, too," old Christopher Lewis added with a shake of his long beard.

"What does it matter who we choose as our leader?" Aunty objected. "This is our coven."

"It didn't matter when the White Holly witches were hidden from the world," Stanford said. "But Esmeralda is right to a point. You do need a strong leader who can hold herself in this modern world when anyone or anything can come for you."

"What would you have us do then, Diesel." Mom sounded hopeful. She'd obviously be fine with anything that didn't involve Maisie going to Louisiana.

But her courage was suddenly failing her at whatever the warlock might suggest, praying it would not have her leave her beloved small town.

"She will go to Montreal."

Damn.

"What?" Mom blurted.

Maisie stood speechless, her mouth wide open with shock.

"From what I hear," Diesel explained, "St-Amand

saved her last night. She can return the favor. As a courtesy to the new members of our Order."

"Courtesy?" Mag grimaced while his brothers remained eerily quiet.

"While I agree that Magnovald has the right to his artifact collection, I understand the Davenport's weariness of letting Emmeline Dubois roam free after what she did to their great-niece. The female vampire needs to be supervised by someone outside her immediate circle."

Emmeline Dubois. Oh shit. Had Maisie heard correctly?

"You want Maisie to go watch over this female predator?" Mom recoiled in disbelief. "The Vampire of Ville-Marie?"

"For a while. To ensure she won't be a threat to anyone."

"So, you're basically sending us a babysitter," Mag snarked.

"I think it's a splendid idea," Nana said. "Maisie will also learn about the vampires' ways. This will make her a fit leader for our coven."

"Wait, Mother," Maisie's mom protested. "She can't leave."

"She has to, Clara," Nana said. "She needs to get out from under your wing. You protect her too much. I'm sure the St-Amands will look after her."

"Maisie." Her grandmother turned to her with a closed expression, her stately bearing fitting of her rank. "You will have to complete this task before I can deem you worthy to take my place."

Maisie gulped, her mind racing at the sudden change of plans.

"Those immortals shouldn't help her one bit," Esmeralda grumbled. "She will have to keep this Dubois beast in check by herself, kill her if needed be."

"No one is killing anyone," Mag blurted. But Valerian had still not said a word.

"You all agree, then," Diesel confirmed to Esmeralda and the others. "You will accept the White Holly witches' choice of new leadership if Maisie completes her task."

Esmeralda remained tight-lipped while the Davenport sisters nodded along with the druid.

"Then it's settled," Diesel proclaimed, his tone allowing no protest. He turned to the immortals. "St-Amands?"

Valerian hadn't spoken since the topic of her rescue had come up. Maisie tried to catch his gaze, but he was silently studying Diesel.

She wondered if he now regretted helping her. If he hadn't saved her, he would be on his way home with minimal commitment to the Order of the Black Oak. But now, he was stuck with her.

"In five months," he finally said, his voice cutting. "Not before."

"Five months?" Diesel frowned.

"Yes. I have Evan to wean first," he said.

Esmeralda turned a calculating eye to Diesel. "Wouldn't that give them time to whisk the Dubois vampire away?"

"December," Valerian stated, daring anyone to say otherwise. "Emme will be there."

Diesel shrugged. "Then it's settled. Maisie will go to Montreal for the winter. She'll report back to us next summer."

Mumbles and nods circulated throughout the crowd, leaving Maisie a nervous wreck. Aware of her turmoil, Mom rose to give Maisie her seat.

With her legs shaky, she sat down in the chair. Her mother's hand on her shoulder did little to calm her. She tried to reason that it would have been worse if she'd gone to Louisiana where the witches would likely try killing her. And Montreal was much closer to home.

"Oh shit, coz, aren't you excited?" Ava murmured down to her.

As the council moved on to other topics, Maisie turned a hesitant brow to her cousin. "A whole winter," she hushed back. "Away from Berwick Hollow."

"You dodged a huge bullet there," Ava added. "Esmeralda is one cruel witch. She would have made your life hell."

With her chest deadened, Maisie ruminated over the trip ahead. Leaving her home, traveling to a different country. It had to be crazy cold up there in December. And what about this Emmeline Dubois.

Dammit, she had read all about the immortal vampire the night before. Not only was the female said to be deadly, but she was Valerian's fiancée.

Valerian who turned her into a pool of need every time his eyes rested on her. She fretted, filled with anxiety as she tuned out the rest of the meeting. She was jolted out only when Ava gave her a small kick in the shin.

She looked up and saw that everyone had left, her mother bringing the rear with the attractive selkie matron.

"He's coming in our direction," Ava warned.

Oh cripes. Her cousin was right. The immortal was closing in on her, his dog jollily flapping his tail as he padded on the grass.

"Good luck." Ava winked at her and silently made her way past him to join the rest of the parley heading into town.

Valerian's pet jogged to her while she remained seated, an uncontrollable flush of heat rising to her cheeks. The handsome canine sniffed her hands and she stopped wringing them to pat his head. His tail again wagged with excitement before he finally sat in front of her.

Well aware of the dog's owner—his clean and spicy scent folding over her and making her swoon—she scratched the back of the animal's ear as he placed his furry head on her lap.

"Good dog." She attempted to calm her racing heart, self-conscious of the immortal staring at her.

"He likes you." Valerian's rich tone echoed above her.

She craned her neck at him to take in his whole height. Her heart trembled to have him so close.

He just stood there, looking at her silently, with a barely visible curl to his mouth.

Was he annoyed that she was coming to his city, or simply amused by her existence? He was, after all, over three hundred years old.

"Thank you," she finally said, digging her fingers in his dog's soft chocolate fur. "For saving me yesterday."

She wanted to let him know she was grateful. But she also needed to understand where she stood with him, find out if he held animosity for her arrangement imposed upon him.

He shrugged casually. "That was nothing."

"But it was," she insisted. "I know what that troll bile does. I would have been unrecognizably burned if I had survived."

The smoldering look he trailed over her caught her by surprise. Was he appraising her body in the flimsy white dress? The thought sent her pulse racing further.

"I'm afraid my rescue caused your coven some trouble," he said.

"Oh, bloody witch politics," she snapped, trying to mask the growing lust at her core.

He smiled fully at her now. "Not political, then?"

"No, not at all," she insisted. "I'm all about the magical craft."

"Then you'll make a fine leader." Still grinning, his eyes lit with an inner glow.

"Not the way my grandmother is." She couldn't help but share her most intimate concerns. There was something about him that made her feel safe. "I'm sorry they all pushed me on you and your home."

"I'm not sorry at all. It will be my pleasure to show you around."

The way he said it, she positively tingled.

"And Miss Dubois?" She was dying to hear about his connection to the infamous vampire.

"Oh, she'll be no trouble. Don't worry."

"Right." She swallowed, not sure what else to say. The tension she felt at his near presence was unmistakable.

He bent down to her and offered his hand to help her rise from the chair. She lay her fingers in his palm and it was as if an electric current had run straight into her. She gulped as the heated shiver trailed along her forearm to scatter all over her sensitive skin.

"It truly would have been a tragedy if any of that troll sap had hurt you." His voice had turned to a low, sexy purr now. "I'm very glad I got you out of the way. Even if it did cause trouble. Would be a shame to destroy such charm."

"And my assigned task?" She rose from her chair, still stunned that she was actually holding his hand after spending a whole night dreaming about it. "Doesn't it bother you?"

"We'll figure something out." A gusty breeze whipped up and he gently removed a leaf that had landed on her head. He caught a lock of her hair and held it a beat too long as his gaze connected with hers. "I'll be happy to welcome you to my home. Dress warmly."

"December," she croaked, her mind and body a dizzying mix of confused feelings.

"Soon." He gently released her hand, leaving her with a deep void at her heart.

"Five months." It seemed so far away.

"See you in Montreal, *ma belle*."

"Montreal, yes," she breathed in reply. "Mr. St-Amand."

With one last penetrating look, he tapped the side of his powerful thigh to call his dog to his side. He turned away from her and took a few strides across the mossy grass before stopping to stare at her over his strapping shoulder.

She bit her lip with a profound desire to run after him and lay a hand at the middle of his wide back. Keep him here with her just a little longer.

As if he sensed her thought, he cast her a heated gaze full of untold promises.

"Mademoiselle Thibodeau." His eyes were like a firing blaze igniting her turmoil. "It's Val. You can call me Val."

Oh cripes.

Dazed with pent-up needs and utter bewilderment, she stood there rooted on the spot in the middle of the clearing, watching the tall figure of the immortal leaving her.

As he disappeared into the woods of her forest with his dog at his heels, she drew a hand to her heated chest, wondering how a complete stranger had managed to turn her world upside down so easily.

She slowly exhaled with anticipation, the silky fabric of her dress gently shifting on her skin along with the fragrant midsummer night.

"Val." His name on her tongue made her dizzy with desire. Filled with longing, the warmth of his touch still lingering on her fingers, she whispered his name in the evening breeze. "Soon, Val. I'll see you again, very soon."

Dear Reader,

You may notice that, unlike my other books, this story ends with a Happy for Now, and not my usual Happily Ever After. Since this is the prequel to Maisie and Val's story, I do hope you will forgive me. I have been mentioning this parlay so many times in the Vampires of the Black Oak series, that I really wanted to see it on the page.

This story comes straight out of my experience as someone who was born and lived in Montreal, and later moved to Narragansett, Rhode Island, as an adult where I lived for seven years. I still miss New England and really wanted to spend a little more time there. Creating a coven of witches in the area was the perfect way for me to do this. And, if you don't mind my sharing a little early news with you, this is not the last time you will encounter Ava Beaudry. Maisie's spunky cousin is planned to be the heroine of her own series eventually. Make sure to check my website often (or join my Secret Circle) to get the latest on that.

Speaking of my Secret Circle, if you are not a member yet and want to be part of my writing process, see how my own heritage has a way of seeping into my writing, and discover which new tortured hero will finally find his true love, I invite you to join where you will receive about two emails a month (usually on Mondays) with my latest progress, small giveaways and freebie reads.

You can join me here: www.subscribepage.com/mcbourque and as a thank you gift for your lovely support, you will receive your own exclusive copy of my American Title winner novel Ancient Whispers, *where the elusive First Witch Morag Callan first makes her appearance into my world.*

A true soulmate story and inspired by the ply of Acadians and Cajuns in North America, this award-winning novel, currently unavailable anywhere, will touch your soul, I promise.

Trust your heart…

Marie-Claude xoxo

. . .

*PS: If you're like me, you might be super curious to finally see Val and Maisie get their Happily Ever After. Read on because I am treating you to a sneak peek into **Book 1 of the Vampires of the Black Oak Series** with Maisie finally meeting her rival, the elusive vampire Emmeline Dubois.*

Will Maisie be able to keep the sassy vampire in check? And is Val still in love with his ex-fiancée?

Keep reading to experience the thrill of Maisie's arrival to Val's home on a frigid Montreal night.

A VAMPIRE'S SPELL
A Witch-Vampire Slow-Burn
Paranormal Romance

Son of an ancient vampire and a legendary French witch, guilt-ridden Mont-Royal Immortal Valerian St-Amand must team with a powerful New England witch to protect his city from a crazed scientist seeking immortality. But as his well-guarded heart softens for Maisie Thibodeau, their quest to eradicate true evil from the streets of Montreal destroys any hope of everlasting love.

Read on for a taste of *A Vampire's Spell*…

A VAMPIRE'S SPELL PREVIEW

Old-Montreal, Québec, Canada
Present Time

Maisie Thibodeau silently eyed the tall blonde vampire who was leaning on the stone wall of the *Sanctuaire des Truands*.

"Are you it?" The deadly woman sneered under Maisie's appraisal. The fur collar of her long deerskin coat fluttered in the icy wind. "You're all they sent to contain me?"

The creature pushed herself to her feet and blocked Maisie's path to the curved porch leading into the historical building. Steadying the heels of her thigh-high leather boots on the packed snow of the courtyard, she crossed her arms at her chest with hostility.

Weary, Maisie hiked her travel duffel bag over her plain down vest. Every inch of her magic legacy soared in her veins as she shot the woman a lethal look.

She would not let Emmeline Dubois rattle her.

Maisie had been chosen to do one job—been sent by

the Order of the Black Oak all the way to Montreal from her small New England town of Berwick Hollow for a single purpose—babysit the unstable vampire. And that was what she would do.

Her fists tightened in her fleece mittens as her mind fixated on her charge. Unknown to the Order, she was also dead set on learning as much as she could about the lethal beings inhabiting the city. Only then would her knowledge of the otherworldly be found vast enough to take over the high priestess-hood of her coven from her grandmother when the time came.

She had big shoes to fill and this assignment would finally convince the supernatural council of the Order that despite her social challenges, Maisie was strong enough to carry on the tradition after Nana Thibodeau.

"Where's your leader, hun?" Maisie's tone was as cold as the air surrounding them. She lifted her chin to level with the vampire's pristine blue gaze, unfettered by the beauty's belligerent attitude.

And yes, Emmeline *was* gorgeous. Tall and perfectly proportioned, her body an ideal hourglass in the trendy formfitting minidress under the pelt coat, her facial features exquisite in their femininity.

But the centuries-old French-Canadian was also a monster. A filthy predator who had a tendency to prey on humans instead of feeding on the synthetic blood offered by the shelter to the cursed ones like her.

And that wretched being was now blocking Maisie's entry to the *Sanctuaire*, an ancient nunnery that was Emmeline's home. Said to have been founded in secret by Saint Marguerite d'Youville in the sixteenth century to help troubled youths, it was now a cleverly disguised haven for newly cursed vampires, the shelter run by none other than Valerian Callan St-Amand, the Mount-Royal Immortal.

Maisie's insides bristled as she searched the courtyard of the sanctuary behind Emmeline, remembering the ancient legacy vampire who'd caught her eye in Berwick Hollow last summer. Valerian St-Amand was nothing like the monster facing Maisie.

"He's got no time for you, *p'tite fille*." Emmeline smirked and took a step forward. A flash of lethal fangs shone beneath the perfectly drawn curve of her lips.

Maisie sighed and cast another anxious look at the entrance, her mouth pursed with apprehension at meeting him again. Then she gripped the handle of her duffel bag tighter. It seemed she would need to deal with her ward before having a chance to meet Valerian to sort out her duties.

"Tell him I'm here," she finally ordered the female vamp, her flat furry boots solidly planted on the icy pavement, her breath leaving tiny crystals of condensation that gleamed under the streetlights illuminating the tortuous empty Old-Montreal street.

"Why?"

"You know perfectly well why, Emmeline Dubois," she spat. "We have an agreement. My nana and Valerian St-Amand. I'm here to watch over you."

The vamp advanced again, her long coat wide open flapping behind her. She was now so close Maisie could smell her expensive perfume and feel the growl that emanated from somewhere inside the creature's belly.

She looked like a fashion model, all right. With her high cheekbones, feline-like features, and her long crystal blonde hair escaping from a luxurious fur hat, no doubt she had ensnared much human prey with that look.

But it was that small cold part of Maisie—that part which made her useless to hold a regular job and unable to read social cues—that made her the perfect guardian for the monster. She would never fall for Emmeline's immense charms.

And of course, Maisie had the magic. As a witch of the White Holly, of those who tethered between sanity and madness, she was fully aware of her abilities to keep the cold beauty in check.

But she really didn't feel like enacting her powers just now.

She reluctantly craned her neck up at the predator and took a resigned step back in a loose defensive pose. Her right hand drew back behind her, her palm prickling with contained energies.

Fighting Emmeline was truly the last thing she wanted to do. She'd had a long bus ride over to Montreal, leaving Berwick Hollow at dawn that morning. It was now past dinnertime; she was hungry and cranky. Her hair felt clammy under the knitted cap, her body stiff from being cramped in a back seat rank with body odor from the over-heated vehicle.

She had expected that someone from the sanctuary would be waiting for her at the bus station. If not Valerian himself, then maybe Father Grégoire who ran the shelter with him.

But as she'd stepped off the bus at the busy downtown station, her blood pounding at the anticipation of finally meeting him again, she had realized they had forgotten her.

Her heart crushed, she had quickly understood that her big assignment—her chance to prove that she was more than a political pawn between vampires, warlocks, and witches—was likely inconsequential to the worldly immortal.

"I never wanted you here, *sorcière*." Emmeline's crystalline blue eyes peered down at Maisie with scorn.

"It's not like you have a choice, is it?" Maisie shot back,

still disappointed that she'd been forgotten, but ready to show her charge who was boss.

"Go home, you stupid bitch," Emmeline drawled with resentment. "Val doesn't want you here."

A VAMPIRE'S SPELL is available on all storefronts.
—find it on your favorite store today!

A FREE STORY FOR YOU…

Enjoyed A Vampire's Heart? Not ready to stop reading
yet? A copy of *ANCIENT WHISPERS*, the harrowing
award-winning story of Gabriel and Lily, Celtic soulmates
reunited in modern time, is yours to download as a thank
you for joining my Secret Circle.
Get your download code at:
marieclaudebourque.com/ancient-whispers

ANCIENT WHISPERS
A Steamy Celtic Soulmate
Paranormal Romance

Gabriel is the youngest member of the Priory of Callan—
an ancient Celtic brotherhood of cursed sorcerers and
alchemists, each with deadly abilities and each haunted by
a tragic past. Tortured by the devastating loss of his fiancée
in 1755, Gabriel wants nothing more than to reunite with
his soul mate.

Two and a half centuries later, Gabriel is still searching for
his love. And then he finds Lily Bellefontaine. Cool-headed
and practical, she has no memory of Gabriel. But she also
can't deny the pull of attraction drawing her under his
seductive spell, urging her to give in to the…
ANCIENT WHISPERS

Read on for a taste of *ANCIENT WHISPERS*…

ANCIENT WHISPERS PREVIEW

"Did you mind celebrating Yule instead of Christmas when you were a child?" Lily asked him. "I mean, it must be difficult being different."

Gabriel smiled back at her as he picked a few snowflakes off her hair. "I celebrated Christmas, just like you. I only met Iain when I was in my twenties."

"Oh yes, for a minute there I thought you were a normal boyfriend. I forget that when you were a child, it was what, seventeen hundred something?" She was still having a hard time trying to adjust to his immortality.

"I was born in 1733 and we did have Christmas, or Noël, as we called it. But now, I just drop by Morag and Iain's at Yule time if I'm around, but honestly, after so many years, the holidays just kind of blend into one another."

"Angèle calls it Noël too sometimes. I just love this time of year. I already set up a tree in the apartment—you have to see it. It's so big Angèle had to help me carry it up the stairs." Lily stopped him in front of the toy store. A model train ran around an adorable miniature village. At the back, a huge castle had been filled with knight and princess figurines. "I was so into damsels in distress and shiny knights in armor as a kid."

"Well, my damsel. May I pledge my allegiance to you?" Gabriel had that twinkle in his eye again, making her laugh. He turned back to the display. "I love that train set. When we have a little boy, that will be his first Christmas present."

Her heart beat faster at the mention of *we*. "So you'll celebrate Christmas when you have kids?"

"When we have kids," he added, making her heart melt. "We'll celebrate both. It will be a great reason for me to have Christmas again."

*You probably wonder about some of the characters you met here…
such as Diesel Stanford, Malcolm Dunsmuir and Harper Grant—as
well as what happens to Val's five brothers and Emmeline Dubois.*

*Here is the list of books current and to-be-released in the Black
Oak world:*

~ *Vampires of the Black Oak* ~

**A Vampire's Heart (Val and Maisie's first meet
cute)**: In this prequel to A Vampire's Spell, awkward witch
Maisie Thibodeau must prove her worth as leader to her
coven by battling a horrible monster in front of the whole
supernatural community.

A Vampire's Spell (Val and Maisie): Guilt-ridden
legacy vampire Valerian St-Amand teams with powerful
witch Maisie Thibodeau to protect his city from a crazed
scientist seeking immortality.

A Vampire's Sin (Mag and Nyssa): Immortal Montreal vampire Mag St-Amand teams up with ambitious real
estate tycoon Nyssa Vlahos to rescue her kid sister from a
child-trafficking ring run by a pack of daemons.

A Vampire's Soul (Emme and Justin): When female
vampire Emmeline Dubois teams up with faithful

immortal friend Justin St-Amand to escape a vicious hunter set to kill her, the centuries-old friendship turns into so much more than she'd anticipated.

A Vampire's Fate (Ren and Rosalie): When female wolf-shifter Rosalie Gauthier returns to her town to take on the leadership of her pack after her father's illness, her birthright is challenged by a tyrannic rival and marriage to powerful vampire Ren St-Amand is her only option to save her family's legacy.

A Vampire's Star (Cass and Tilly) Can an immortal truly father a child? That's what rock star Cass St-Amand finds out when Tilly Davenport, a strong-headed music producer banshee, shows up backstage at his latest concert claiming to be carrying his child.

A Vampire's Blood (Griff and Isabelle) Can you fall in love with your lifelong enemy? Griff St-Amand has his hands full when he finds himself having to rescue French supernatural hunter Isabelle LeGall despite her hatred for his family.

~ Warlocks of the Black Oak ~

A Warlock's Kiss (Diesel and Kera): Stoic warlock leader Diesel Stanford must convince his panther-shifter ex-girlfriend Kerala Clarke to return the only magical artifact that can cure his sister from a terrible hex.

A Sorcerer's Night (Sin and Celeste): Protective panther-shifter sorcerer Sinclair Clarke battles a powerful demon who holds hostage his fiancee, legacy witch Celeste Stanford.

An Alchemist's Desire (Thorn and Raven): Recluse alchemist Thornwood Huntington must help talented violinist Raven Giancola unlock the magic of her enchanted violin despite his vow to keep all things magic away from non-sorcerers.

An Archmage's Destiny (Knight and Bryce): With her reputation on the line, steadfast attorney Bryce Jackson must convince daredevil warlock Knightley Morgan to return to the folds of his powerful New England family or apply the devastating consequences herself.

A Spellbinder's Denial (Duke and Sloane): Riddled with guilt after his unleashed powers wrecked lives decades ago, billionaire warlock Duke Morgan still refuses to unlock his powers to make amends, but when savvy banshee Sloane Davenport crosses his path again, even his fortune won't be enough to protect her.

A Necromancer's Love (Mal and Harper): When vampires descend on his city, Seattle necromancer Malcolm Dunsmuir can no longer hide from the darkness of his demon side, especially when the enticing life-loving human Harper Grant tries her very best to bring him to the light.

A Warlock's Storm (Rey and Saira): Stranded on a boat in a haunted New England harbor, rugged warlock Rey Stanford and sassy female panther-shifter Saira Varma battle sea-monsters and revenants as they try to survive the night.

CAST OF MAIN CHARACTERS

Vampires:

Valerian (Val) St-Amand: Mount-Royal Immortal and founder of the *Sanctuaire des Truands* shelter in Montreal. Brother to Mag, Justin, Ren, Cass and Griff.

Magnovald (Mag) St-Amand: Mount-Royal Immortal and owner of the *Serpent Maudit* night club in Montreal. Brother to Val, Justin, Ren, Cass and Griff.

Professor Justinien (Justin) St-Amand: Mount-Royal Immortal and professor of Astronomy at McDougall College in Montreal. Brother to Val, Mag, Ren, Cass and Griff

Renaud (Ren) St-Amand: Mount-Royal Immortal and honorary member of the Domaine-Lassale Wolf Pack.

Cassiodore (Cass) St-Amand: Mount-Royal Immortal and brother to Val, Mag, Justin, Ren and Griff.

Griffon (Griff) St-Amand: Mount-Royal Immortal and brother to Val, Mag, Justin, Ren and Cass.

Emmeline (Emme) Dubois: Montreal immortal vampire and former fiancée of Val St-Amand. Friend to the St-Amand brothers.

Evan Grant: cursed Montreal vampire, sister to the Daemon Queen Harper Grant, and bouncer to Mag St-Amand. Was saved from blood addiction by Val St-Amand and the *Sanctuaire des Truands* shelter.

Witches:

Maisie Thibodeau: Witch of the White Holly Coven in Berwick Hollow

Ava Beaudry: White Holly witch and cousin of Maisie Thibodeau

Clara Thibodeau: White Holly empath and mother of Maisie Thibodeau.

High Priestess Marianne Thibodeau: High Priestess of the While Holly Coven in Berwick Hollow and grandmother to Maisie Thibodeau

The Elder Agatha Beaudry: Immortal elder of the White Holy Coven and distant relative to the Thibodeaus in Berwick Hollow

Marla Thibodeau: White Holly witch and cousin of Maisie Thibodeau

Taylor Marquis: White Holly witch and friend of Maisie Thibodeau

Esmeralda Deveraux: High Priestess of the Waxing Crescent Coven in Louisiana. Rival of the White Holly witches.

Charlotte Callan (aka The Ice Witch): Ancient witch of the Callanish tradition and mother of the Mount-Royal Immortals.

Warlocks:

Diesel Stanford: Warlock and leader of the Order of the Black Oak. Resides in Seaport with his wife panther-shifter Kerala Clarke and their young son Sai Stanford.

Celeste Stanford: Witch of the Black Oak. Sister to Diesel Stanford and resides in Seaport with her husband, panther-shifter Sinclair Clarke

Sinclair Clarke: Warlock of the Black Oak and panther-shifter. Brother to Kerala Clarke Stanford. Resides in Seaport with his wife Celeste Stanford.

Disciples of Nostredame:

Father Grégoire: Oldest disciple of Nostredame, living at the *Sanctuaire des Truands* in Montreal and assigned to Val St-Amand

Faithful Companion:

Sasha: Chocolate Labrador dog and devoted companion to Val St-Amand

Daemons:

King Malcolm (Mal) Dunsmuir: Warlock of the Black Oak, Necromancer and King of the Daemon Realm. Consort to Harper Grant.
Queen Harper Grant: Queen of the Daemon Realm, consort to Mal Dunsmuir and sister to cursed vampire Evan Grant.

Banshees:

April and June Davenport: elderly banshee sisters residing in the Pacific Northwest. Great-aunts of Baby Elsa Davenport and friends of Malcolm Dunsmuir

Humans:

Chelsea Jones: Assistant to billionaire warlock Duke Morgan and leader of the Black Oak Huntsmen
Jesse Sullivan: Human police officer residing in Berwick Hollow and promised to witch Ava Beaudry

FRENCH-ENGLISH GLOSSARY

mon frère – *my brother*
ma belle - *beautiful*
Madame - *Madam*
Nouvelle-France – *New France*
Québec – *Quebec City*
Rituel du Sang – *Blood Ritual*
Seigneur - *lord (common French-Canadian curse)*
Serpent Maudit – *Cursed Snake*
sacrament - *sacrament, as in the Christian rite. (Common French Canadian curse)*
Sanctuaire des Truants - *Sanctuary of the Miscreant*
sorcière du Clan de Callan – *witch of the Callan Clan*

ACKNOWLEDGEMENTS

I want to thank all the readers who have followed me through the Order of the Black Oak journey. Thank you all from the bottom of my heart. Your support means the world to me.

I am also very grateful to my faithful accountability parters including Rebecca Rivard, Laura Bickle, Merrie Destephano, Celia Breslin, and the group at Angela James' From Written to Recommended.

I also want to give deep thanks to super talented romance author, friend and my amazing editor Jenn Bray-Webber who helped so much with all my books. Thank you also to Charity Chimni for her eagle-eye proofreading and Frauke Spanuth for a great set of covers.

And last but not least, deepest thanks to my lovely readers Reena, Evelyn, Cheryl, Rain, Cathy, Pauline, Shirl and Mary for their help in naming Val's trustworthy companion Sasha.

Marie-Claude Bourque is an author of gothic paranormal romance and the winner of the American Title V award with her first novel ANCIENT WHISPERS.

Her writing features modern-day fantasy skillfully weaved into infinitely romantic stories between smart strong women and complex passionate heroes.
Happily Ever After always absolutely guaranteed!
Find more at www.marieclaudebourque.com

To be first to hear about her latest book, win free copies and more, subscribe to
Marie-Claude's Secret Circle at
https://marieclaudebourque.com/secret-circle/

Or connect directly with her at
www.facebook.com/mcbourque

facebook.com/mcbourque

twitter.com/mcbourque

amazon.com/author/marieclaudebourque

goodreads.com/mcbourque

bookbub.com/profile/marie-claude-bourque

instagram.com/marie.claude.now